Under Pressure

Barbara Winkes

ISBN: 978-1-0693045-7-5

For D.

Chapter One

C oncerned glances. She could have done without them, but like every morning she came to work, Detective Luce Allen reminded herself that it could be much worse. She had a lot to be grateful for.

She had closed another major case soon after her abduction. The renovations at her home that had been stalled for a long time were finally coming to an end—and then, there was the most wonderful surprise. Luce never allowed herself to think about it too much here at work, where drama and tragedy could intrude at any moment.

Where the concerned glances were an indicator that not everything in her life had been smooth sailing lately.

When she heard laughter, she cast a glance over at where Detectives Ritter and Murphy were standing in the corner, engaged in a joke or maybe some general male bonding. Another surprise that Murphy had decided to join the unit for good, but Luce could live with that.

Ritter, usually stoic, seemed in a good mood this morning. Her partner had been less grumpy in the past few weeks, though Luce hadn't yet decided whether the reason was that she'd saved his life, or Tyler Murphy's transfer. Everything that made her colleagues focus less on her was welcome—so they could all move on with their lives.

So far so good.

She opened the top drawer of her desk, frowning at its contents. Luce closed it soundly enough to make the young officer who had come up to her, flinch.

"Detective? I have someone here who needs to talk to an investigator."

"Thanks. I'm coming."

Luce got up to follow him into the waiting area where a woman in her thirties sat clutching her purse. Nervousness was radiating off of her.

Enough pondering the state of her life—time to work.

"Ma'am? My name is Luce Allen. I'm a Detective with Special Crimes. How can I help you?"

The woman got to her feet, raising tear-filled eyes at her.

"I'm scared something happened to Mrs. Burke. She and her little girl are gone."

"Please come with me."

No doubt about it, other people deserved and needed concern a lot more than Luce did these days. She led the woman to an empty conference room and sat down with her.

"Could you tell me your name, and what happened?"

"Anna Price. I've been working for Mrs. Burke for a couple of years now, and I know she wouldn't just disappear like that!" She took a deep breath. "Initially she hired me for cleaning, but I do a little bit of everything now. Sometimes I watch Poppy too. When I came to the house this morning, they were both gone."

"Are you sure there isn't a harmless explanation? Could they have gone somewhere, and she forgot to tell you?"

She shook her head. "No. Poppy has school, and Mrs. Burke is working. There was breakfast on the table. I can't reach her on the phone. I should have done more." She was crying in earnest, and Luce got up to get a box of tissues she sat in front of the distraught visitor.

"What do you mean by that?" she asked softly.

"She and Poppy had a schedule, and everything had to go according to it. I felt it wasn't my place to ask, but sometimes I thought it made her feel safer. I think there must have been a bad relationship in the past, or something...She is very protective of her daughter."

So far...so many questions. The practical first.

"You have a key I assume?"

"Yes. I locked and came here right away."

That was likely a good decision, but Luce didn't want to upset the woman any more by reminding her that time was ticking.

Anna Price removed the key from her chain and laid it on the table. "Will you go?"

"Yes, we'll look into it," Luce promised. "First, I'd like you to give me your contact information, and Mrs. Burke's address and phone number." She pushed the notepad and pen towards Anna.

"Thank you. Please find her."

Anna held her phone out to Luce after writing down the address in neat handwriting.

"Thanks. One more thing. Are you aware of any threats she might have received recently?"

An interrupted meal still on the table was worrisome in Luce's opinion, but as long as there was no indicator of violence, there was still the hope that the two had left of their own volition.

"Nothing specific, but it often seemed to me that she was ducking. Her whole demeanor, you know what I mean?"

Luce could imagine.

"Is that why you're suspecting a bad relationship?"

"She reminded me of my mother," Anna said. "I didn't need so many words."

"You know anything about Poppy's father?"

"Not much, except that he has money. He sends a few expensive gifts, but I've never met him."

"Okay. Thank you, Ms. Price. We'll be in touch."

Luce had the impression that she was going to meet him soon.

After she'd seen her out, Luce went back inside where Ritter and Murphy had finished their conversation and retreated to their own workspaces. Luce bypassed Murphy's desk and went straight to Ritter's.

"We have a possible abduction, a woman and her eight-year-old daughter. Alternative theory is that she could be running from an abusive ex."

"Pleasant," Ritter commented. "Let's go check it out."

When Anna Price told her the address, Luce knew they'd be visiting a wealthy neighborhood. Still, she was a bit surprised when she opened the door to the two-story house, and they walked inside the space. She didn't want to jump to conclusions about Burke's relationship with Poppy's father. Price had mentioned expensive gifts...Burke could have wealth of her own, but in any case, her location wasn't a secret to the father of her child. If he was the "bad relationship."

"Security cameras outside," Ritter remarked. "Let's hope they were recording."

"Yes. And ideally, we'll find the device they were hooked up to. I'll take downstairs?"

"Sure."

When she walked into the kitchen, she could see what Anna had described: Two plates on the table, coffee gone cold in a cup, chocolate milk in a glass. On the stove sat a pan with scrambled eggs in them. The stove was turned off, and Luce made a note to ask Anna if she had done it.

While nothing spoke of violence at this moment, she could understand the woman's alarm. She went to the calendar on the wall, seeing that it was almost full with multiple appointments and activities. Well planned out.

It might be the way Sarah Burke was coping with the past, or life as a single mother, though to Luce, the detailed descriptions bordered on compulsion. She leaned closer to study the items on the counter, including a jar that held a few twenty-dollar bills.

Definitely not a robbery.

But someone could have come in and convinced her to come with them, threatening her or Poppy—with a gun?

They'd have to find out if Anna's suspicions were more than a hunch, though she feared they might be accurate. In her experience, someone who had experienced trauma often could sense its traces in others.

"It doesn't look like they took any clothes," Ritter said behind her. "The kid's schoolwork is still all over her desk, toiletries in the bathroom...no electronic devices so far, but I found the name of the security company that installed the cameras. They could have backups."

"Let's hope so. I didn't find any devices either," Luce returned. She was hopeful though. If Sarah had paid the company to monitor her home, they might have something that would help them find her.

"So, what's your take?"

"She might have gotten a text or a phone call that made her decide to leave. Her housekeeper gave me her phone number. I checked earlier, but it's off. We can still give it to the lab and see what they can do. My take, based on what Mrs. Price told me—and this schedule..." She pointed to the calendar. "She doesn't seem like someone who'd just get up and walk away in the middle of breakfast."

"Yeah. How often does Price come in?"

"Every other day. We have to check with Burke's workplace, and the school as well. Let's head back and make a few calls."

Sarah Burke's car still sat in the garage, making it even less likely that she had left willingly.

❧

Before noon, Sarah Burke and her daughter Poppy were officially missing. Luce had managed to get the principal of Poppy's school on the phone who confirmed that Poppy hadn't been in school yesterday and this morning.

"We left a message on her voicemail, and at Mrs. Burke's workplace, but we haven't heard back yet."

Luce could practically hear him frown.

"This is worrisome."

She didn't disagree. "To your knowledge, has anything like this ever happened before?"

She could have guessed the answer.

"Not that I can think of. I'm sorry, Detective. You don't think anything happened to them?"

"That's what we're trying to figure out. Do you, by any chance, have the contact information for Poppy's father?"

"Oh." He sounded surprised. "I didn't think he was in the picture. I'm sorry, I can't help you there."

"That's all right. Thanks."

Her call to Sarah Burke's workplace, an architectural firm, was almost a carbon copy—Sarah hadn't come in yesterday or today, and no one had been able to reach her.

Except for her housekeeper, none of the people in question were close enough to show up at her house or make otherwise inquiries after they couldn't reach her on the phone within a certain period of time. No one seemed to know about Poppy's father either.

The breakfast on the table was older than a few hours.

"Checked with the hospitals and the morgue. No sign of her," Ritter told her after she ended the call.

That was a relief, at least the latter.

"I'll get on the cameras next?"

"Yes, do that."

On with the next steps.

Luce tried the number again, to no avail. She spent the next few hours trying to trace Sarah Burke's steps with little success. At least, Ritter did have success with the security company, and they got the call from the lab not much later.

"Hey," she greeted the lab tech. "What do you have for me? Anything from the cameras?"

"Well, that's a bit tricky," the woman said. Disappointment made Luce's stomach flutter, or maybe she'd had too much caffeine. Even when busy, she managed to overdo it—that had been her reality for the past two decades or so.

"What do you mean? They looked new."

"Yes, and that wasn't the problem. They were fairly new, and we got the footage for the time period we needed. Images are clear, but they don't show anyone going in or leaving that house during the timeframe."

"That's impossible."

"Well, that's what we're dealing with. Something interesting about the phone number though. She had a lot of calls from one number recently, called back twice in the past couple of days."

"You know who that is?"

"Normally I'd have to get authorization first, but this one I could look up in the Yellow Pages. It's headquarters of Brock Construction. I tried it and got the reception desk."

"That's...interesting."

"I would have expected a bit more enthusiasm."

"Oh, I'm enthusiastic about it, don't doubt it. Thank you. I think this conversation will be helpful," she told Ritter. "First, let's do some research on Brock Construction."

Chapter Two

Her phone rang when they were in the car. Since Ritter was driving, Luce considered it safe to answer.

"Hey." Kendra's voice was warm and soft, going straight past the professional guard she was used to keeping up at work. Luce cast a quick look at Ritter who was focused on the road. Good.

She suppressed a smile.

"Hey you," she said. "I'm afraid I don't have much time."

"How formal, Detective Allen." Kendra laughed. "I'm between patients, so don't worry, I won't keep you long. I was just wondering if I could pick you up later. I had a cancellation...We could have dinner."

They were still exploring the space between them with caution. Hope, too. So much hope. Luce's answer might have been a different one a few months ago, but she knew that even a long day in her world meant that she might finish early enough for Kendra.

"That sounds great," she admitted. "I'm not sure yet...We have to see how this goes. I'll try, okay?"

"That's good enough for me. Have you eaten anything?"

"Nothing you would be happy about." Luce had no illusions, but all of a sudden, the day was so much better. "We'll talk later?"

"I could come by after I leave here," Kendra offered. "I know my way around."

"Yeah. All right. I'll see you."

It was tough to keep her tone neutral next to her partner, even knowing he wasn't overly curious about her personal life—or at all. They had gotten closer since the dramatic events of their latest cases, but that didn't mean they were friends. Like him and Tyler, apparently.

She caught the small smile on his face before it was gone.

"What?"

"Nothing, Allen. So, Mr. Brick?"

"Brock," she corrected before she realized he wasn't serious. "Brick. Construction. When did you get so funny?"

"Maybe when I survived getting shot. Lighten up a little bit, will you?"

Luce let that one go. At least he hadn't told her to smile more. Even Ritter knew not to go there, not with her, not these days. No matter how happy she was.

"Housekeeper said something about a bad relationship, but she doesn't know the father of the girl, so it could be anyone from Sarah's past—or present, unfortunately. At this point, all we know is that they were divorced two years ago. Anna Price started working for her a little later."

"You think she got the house in the divorce? It's a lot of space for two people."

"I don't know, but I guess we'll find out soon."

They made it to the secretary's desk where the woman in her forties predictably tried to stall her.

"I'm not sure Mr. Brock is available. I could give you an appointment..."

"I think he'll make time," Ritter said, holding up his badge. "Detective Ritter, Special Crimes, this is my colleague Detective

Allen. I think Mr. Brock might prefer to sacrifice a few minutes of his time rather than come to the station?"

At this point, they wouldn't mention to her that this was still an option.

The woman's eyes widened, her cheeks flushing.

"Can I ask what this is about?"

"We'd prefer to discuss it with Mr. Brock himself," Luce answered.

Out of excuses and stalling tactics, the secretary picked up her phone, her tone soft and apologetic.

"I'm so sorry, Mr. Brock, but the police are here. They say they want to talk to you. No, I don't know, they won't tell me. Can I...Yes, thank you, Mr. Brock. You can go in," she said, looking apprehensive.

Mr. Brock came out from behind his massive desk when they entered the office.

"This is unusual," he said, his jovial smile a stark contrast to the secretary's stressed demeanor. He didn't seem all that busy, Luce noticed.

"We're here about your ex-wife," she said, prompting him to laugh.

"Which one?"

She had to admit she hadn't expected that.

"Sarah Burke."

"Oh, all right. Sarah. What do you want to know about her? I haven't had much contact with her in the past two years."

"You have a child though. Poppy."

He frowned.

"Is Poppy all right? Is that why you're here?"

"We don't know. Sarah and Poppy are missing."

"Missing how?" The smile was gone. "I can't believe this! Did she finally go off the deep end? If she hurt my daughter, I'll make sure she's held responsible."

Luce exchanged a quick look with Ritter whose expression was impassive.

"What makes you say that? Are you aware of any problems Sarah might have? Did she ever hurt Poppy?"

"Not physically, I don't think so. But she's definitely troubled, and I think that has been impacting Poppy."

Luce reminded herself that in two years, the housekeeper had never seen the man, didn't know anything about him other than he sent gifts sometimes. Had he misunderstood signs of posttraumatic stress, had he caused them, or did Sarah present a danger to her daughter?

"Troubled how?"

"She needs things to be her way, or she freaks out. She doesn't yell, but she gets very quiet and depressed if you know what I mean. The last time I saw Poppy, I thought she was worried."

"When did you last see her?" Ritter interjected.

"Two months ago, maybe?" He shrugged. "I'm busy. They granted Sarah full custody after the divorce. I wonder how the people in question feel about that now. I'm afraid I don't have any more time. If there's nothing else?"

Ritter's neutral expression slipped a little. Luce could understand why. With the news they had just brought him, Brock was simply going back to work? It made her wonder if his concern was real after all.

"Are you aware of any friends or family Sarah might be with?"

If only they could figure out what had happened with the security camera footage. Luce had the feeling they would come back to that. Could someone have replaced it? Was that too much of a movie plot?

"Sarah didn't have many friends, except for that housekeeper, more like a cleaning lady who came over a few times a week. Her parents are in Montana, but they are estranged."

"Didn't?"

"Figure of speech. When I met her, I meant, and she didn't make a lot during our marriage either. I'm sorry, I have no idea what happened, but I'll make a few calls. If I learn anything, I'll let you know. I hope you'll do the same for me."

"Of course."

Luce handed him her card.

"Don't get me wrong," he said, holding her gaze. "I care about her. We've had some difficult times, but I loved her, and our daughter. I wish they were still in my life other than..." He laughed bitterly. "The occasional encounters of a divorced couple."

"So, Sarah was the one who filed for divorce?" Luce asked.

"I know what you're thinking, and that you have to ask, so I'll save you the time. I have an alibi. I spent all day in my office. My secretary and a whole host of other people will confirm that."

"What about two days ago?" Ritter asked.

"Back-to-back meetings," he returned. "We landed a few huge contracts last week, and I've barely spent any time at home. I have a driver and my staff at home. You'll see, I don't spend a lot of time alone."

"Okay. Thank you for your time, Mr. Brock."

The moment Luce picked up her phone she knew that a romantic relaxed dinner was likely out of the question. She had several messages, and it kept buzzing. Looking over at Ritter, she realized it was the same for him.

With a shrug, she picked up.

"Lieutenant Chomsky. What's going on?"

"Where are you?" She sounded terse.

"We just left Brock's company. The missing woman's ex-husband."

"We have bigger problems," Chomsky informed her grimly. "We have received several calls from parents of students at Carter Academy. So far, six kids, all supposed to be on the same school bus, haven't come home."

"What?" It was the only thing Luce could say without resorting to a curse. Six more kids in addition to Poppy Burke. Maybe more. This day was going to hell fast.

"Hold on, I spoke to the principal this morning. The missing girl, Poppy Burke, goes to the same school."

"Come back here as soon as you can," Chomsky instructed her. "There's a BOLO out on the bus, nothing so far, but we have a lot of terrified parents here."

"I can imagine. We'll be there in fifteen minutes," Luce promised.

After she ended the call, she looked over at Ritter who was scowling at his messages.

"I guess you heard."

"How is that possible? An entire school bus," he muttered. "This had better not be the same shit as Chowchilla."

Luce wholeheartedly agreed with him. "The same school Poppy goes to. It can't be a coincidence."

Ritter shook his head. "This is fucked up."

They had never been this much on the same page.

Chapter Three

When they arrived at the station, a news van was already waiting for them. Several reporters from various news outlets started shouting questions. Once she and Ritter had made it inside the station, she cast an incredulous look over her shoulder.

"How are they already here?"

"Ask your cousin sometime," he said with a wry grin. "I don't think this will be the most difficult part of the day."

Luce assumed that her cousin Jill would be a bit more considerate, but she didn't care to start an argument at this moment. They would have to talk to the parents one by one. She wasn't looking forward to that, the fear, the grief...For once, she would have liked her missing person to be a kid who got lost in the mall and turned up five minutes later. Something along those lines.

Chomsky came out of her office as soon as she saw them.

"We're in the process of setting up a helpline and an area for the parents who are already here."

Luce nodded. "Do we know what happened? Did the bus go off route?"

"We know next to nothing yet," Chomsky answered, clearly frustrated. "No one can reach the driver. There are some traffic cameras in the area."

"I can take care of that," Ritter offered.

"Good. Allen, you and Murphy will speak to the parents. You can use the conference room next to my office."

"Okay." It would be okay. They had worked together under difficult circumstances before and still considered themselves friends.

This was nothing compared to the anguish of the missing children's parents. She thought of the photograph she'd seen in Sarah Burke's living room, of Sarah and eight-year-old Poppy.

All the same age.

All from the same school.

She had an odd feeling about Brock and the things he'd told them concerning Sarah, but she couldn't imagine he'd be responsible for a bus full of children going missing.

～◦～

"I don't understand. It's not even that far! They take the same route every day. How can they be missing?"

"We will figure out what happened," Tyler reassured Leona Dennis, the mother of nine-year-old Justin. She had come with her husband, both of them angry and scared like all the others.

Luce could feel the exhaustion tug at her mind. They had gotten a hold of the principal once more. She was on her way, but first she had given them a list of all the students who were supposed to be on that bus. Twelve altogether.

Heaven help us.

"So, there haven't been any problems before?" Luce asked.

"No, of course not. We know the driver. He's been with the company that the school hires for years, always responsible. He once called when they were stuck in traffic, so we wouldn't worry. If there was an accident, you would know, wouldn't you?" Tears were glistening in her eyes. Her husband laid a hand on her shoulder, and she leaned into him.

"Do you know Sarah Burke?" she asked, and the woman straightened.

"Poppy's mother? Why would you ask that? Do you think her no good ex has something to do with it?"

"You know about her ex?"

"We don't know him personally, if that's what you mean," Mr. Dennis answered. "But Justin once went over to their house with some other kids, for Poppy's birthday party. He came by when we were picking up Justin, and I swear, Sarah just wanted to disappear. She was like a different person. He left, and she sort of switched back. Justin never went back."

He fixed her with a stern gaze. "Are you going to look into that?"

"We are following all leads." Luce could imagine this was a worthwhile one, but the question remained: What use could Brock have for a school bus full of kids? He might want Sarah and Poppy back in his life, though Luce wasn't too sure about Sarah.

A knock on the door proceeded Lieutenant Chomsky into the room.

"Detective Allen? A moment?"

Luce couldn't be more grateful. Tyler was better at this anyway. However, her supervisor's soft tone troubled her.

"Bad news?" she asked.

"The principal is here. Ritter is still working on the traffic cams, so I'd like you to talk to him."

"Of course."

Outside, daylight was fading. Luce wondered what the morning would bring. She had resigned to the fact that this case had taken on dimensions no one could have imagined a few hours ago.

"This is a horrible development." Principal Steyer had chosen to stand rather than take the seat offered. "Please tell me you are making progress on finding these children."

"I was hoping you could help us with that. A few of the parents mentioned the driver. No one has been able to reach him yet, but I imagine you have some information?"

"On Matt? Of course, but he hasn't been driving that bus in a couple of days. He called in sick Monday morning."

"What about his replacement?"

"Mr. Reilly. I tried to reach him as well. His phone is turned off."

Same for the children's phones. Luce couldn't hide her surprise when she learned how many of the students had them. The thought that most of them weren't much older than her niece Josie was uncomfortable.

"You know him as well? The parents seemed familiar with Mr. Layne."

"Right, Matt's been the driver on this route for a long time. Reilly, doesn't ring a bell."

"Okay. I need everything you have on him, address, phone number, and could you get hold of someone at the company?"

"Now?" He looked doubtful. "Their offices must be closed at this time."

"Try anyway. Please," she added. No need to add to the already sky-high tension. "Could you wait here for a moment? I'll be right back."

Luce found Ritter who was frowning at traffic camera footage. A team had been assembled to investigate this avenue, but from the terse atmosphere, she could guess they didn't have any success yet.

18

"Look at this," he said, sounding frustrated as he played a part for her. "Here, they are just a couple of miles away from the school. After that, nothing."

"That's not possible."

"My point exactly."

It was impossible. The bus couldn't just vanish.

"If this isn't solved by tomorrow at this time, someone will start talking alien abduction," he muttered.

"If this isn't solved by tomorrow at this time, we'll have bigger problems," she commented. "You keep at this. Tyler and I will look into the driver as soon as he's done talking to the parents, and we will check out the route on the way."

"Good idea." Lieutenant Chomsky was everywhere tonight. "We sent a team already, go meet with them as soon as possible."

"Detectives." The principal had not heeded her advice and followed her back into the squad room. "I'm sorry. I thought you would want to know right away." He looked pale, and Luce braced herself. "They're closed, but I know someone at the company. They're not that big, so they were able to tell me right away. They claim that they never sent Mr. Reilly. In fact, he's on a month-long vacation at the moment."

Luce said out loud what she assumed everyone to be thinking.

"Then who was driving the damn bus?"

※

"This has to be torture. Can you imagine waiting for your kid, they don't come home, and you have no idea what happened—I'm sorry," Tyler said, probably realizing that these subjects—kids, torture—were far from just shop talk between the two of them.

"I prefer not to imagine any of it," she returned. "What we have is bad enough. Someone planned this, got the other guy in. We have to talk to Matt Layne as well."

"Tonight?"

"The parents seem to think he cares a lot about those kids. If that's true he won't mind us waking him up."

"True. What do we know about this other guy so far?"

"Had the paperwork to show to the school, drove Monday with no incident, and today, the bus disappeared. He's not answering his phone, but he gave this address with the papers."

"Let me guess. Not the real Frank Reilly's address either."

"I don't think so. The principal doesn't know where the real Reilly went on vacation, but maybe someone at the bus company knows. He could be in on it. I sent someone to the house of the principal's contact..." She checked the name on her phone. "Beckett. Not sure if they know anything, but it's worth a try."

"All right. Let's see what we can find at fake Mr. Reilly's," Tyler suggested.

They had arrived, and for the second time that day, Luce found herself in a missing person's home, though the circumstances differed greatly.

The sights were just as alarming: The apartment was mostly empty. A map of the city on the wall in the sparsely furnished living room. In the bedroom, they found a mattress with a blanket on the floor. Whoever had stayed here didn't intend to make it long.

"Damn. I don't suppose he left us any electronics."

Luce opened all the closets. Empty hangers, no toiletries in the bathroom. The man impersonating Frank Reilly was gone.

"We need someone to go over this with a fine-toothed comb. If he's been living here for a few days, there's got to be something. I doubt that they had time to clean it all up."

Tyler stepped towards the map, and she followed him.

Nothing was marked, but they could easily find the school's address, about ten minutes from where they were now.

"There are some wooded areas, but in order to get there, they would have passed traffic cams here...and here," Luce said. "There's no way."

She was reminded of another impossible coincidence: The security cameras at Sarah Burke's house, not giving them any clue as to when she and her daughter had left the house, and with whom—but they had been running.

"Let's finish up here and meet the team," he suggested.

"Yeah, let's do that."

Chapter Four

S he was tired, but Luce wanted to make sure they had put every possible measure in place before she could even think of taking a break. Her stomach was in knots. It might be the pressure getting to her. It might be that it hadn't gotten much besides coffee, and that wouldn't change anytime soon.

They drove to Carter Academy and followed the route of the school bus from there. Squad cars were scattered alongside the road, but so far, none of their colleagues had turned up anything. The closer they got to the location where the bus had last been caught on camera, the more the tension settled in her shoulders. They couldn't go back and face those parents empty-handed.

It wasn't like she'd never had to do it before, but nothing of this scale. Tonight, of all nights, Luce wasn't sure she could handle it.

"We will have to send those parents home. Get the information out to the press. There's not much else we can do tonight, unless something comes up..." He cast her a quick sideways glance as if to gauge her reaction. Their teamwork was just fine, Luce reflected. Something to be relieved about, even though the day hadn't brought much else.

"We can't go home like this."

"Not yet, but if I spend the night, I need some food," he declared. "You'd like to find a diner later?"

She made a non-committal sound as she stared out the window. It was dark now, the probability that they'd find something getting lower by the minute. They were now driving through the wooded area they'd seen on the map in Reilly's apartment a short while ago.

There had to be prints on that map. Wishful thinking?

"Take this road? We can swing by Matt Layne's before going back to the station."

Tyler cast her a doubtful glance but he took the turn. "I don't know what you're hoping to find. Isn't it more important to talk to Layne—"

"On second thought, let's send someone else to Layne. I'll check where Ritter is at. I want to spend some more time around here. They must have come this way."

"Luce, you're tired."

"There's no other way. If they took any other road, the cameras would have caught them. The city was cutting branches a few streets down last week, because they were starting to cover signs."

"I know what you mean, but what are the odds that vegetation took out the only camera that would have caught where the bus was going?" He frowned. "It's not exactly the terrain to drive a bus."

"But lots of space to hide one. Let's just take a look, and if all else fails, we'll come back tomorrow."

Her phone rang, on the other end an apologetic Kendra.

"I'm so sorry, there was an emergency. Rain check on dinner?"

Luce was both disappointed and relieved that she wasn't the one canceling. She realized Kendra might not have heard the news yet if she'd been busy with patients non-stop.

"No problem. I'm tied up here as well."

"Okay. Perhaps on the weekend?"

"Sure. I'm sorry, I have to go."

She and Kendra still had some things to figure out beyond a rushed dinner between work shifts. They'd make time after this out-of-control day. Someday. For now, she had to bring a dozen children back to their parents.

The road leading up into the woods would indeed be challenging for the bus. They got out of the car, examining the area with flashlights.

Luce wasn't sure if the tire tracks would tell a story, because people came up here for work and leisure, some with bigger trucks. Reality was catching up with her quickly, though she couldn't help thinking of what Ritter had said earlier. What if the perpetrators had been inspired by another, infamous school bus kidnapping?

But what was their endgame?

"If they were going for a ransom, we'd know already," she said out loud. They walked a bit further, until Tyler said, "How about we head back, see if there's anything to take care of right now, and we get something to eat?"

"Yes, in a minute." She moved her flashlight over the huge trees lining the road until something caught her attention. Something yellow. She took a closer look at the flakes caught in the tree bark. "Look. Yellow paint."

His expression was somber.

"They came around here. Let's get the car, and call it in."

"There are a few businesses around here, a motel if I'm not mistaken, some ongoing construction. I think they were talking about deforesting in this area?"

Construction. Brock. There was a tape running in the back of her mind. She couldn't forget about Sarah and Poppy. It didn't make sense that the two cases were related, and yet those disappearances happening on the same day couldn't be a coincidence.

The forest didn't give up its secrets easily either.

They'd been driving for ten more minutes, then fifteen, without any trace of the elusive bus.

"How have you been doing?" Tyler asked, out of the blue.

"Same as the past few weeks. Okay. I'd feel better if we could bring this to an end soon."

"Yeah."

Luce appreciated that he cared, but it was neither the time nor the place to go into details, not that she ever wanted to. In the aftermath, she had achieved a balance, still fragile, but a balance. Kendra had a lot to do with that.

This case would be somewhat of a test, though she had caught a predator running a human trafficking ring soon after her return to work. She was okay, as much as she could be.

They got out of the car again when they came across flattened bushes on the side of the road, where a path had been forged by a large vehicle. Luce and Tyler got out on foot once more, not to destroy any possible evidence.

Another ten minutes of walking deeper into the woods before their flashlights caught another flash of yellow.

Luce's stomach lurched.

<hr />

"Good work," Chomsky commented once they had returned to the station for a quick briefing. "Wrap up here for today. I'll get the night shift on this, and we're going to take the bus to forensics right now. Another team has gone back to Frank Reilly's house. We will have some results soon."

Luce wasn't sure if Chomsky's speech was fueled by anything other than determination. But finding the bus was a big step. A helicopter was flying over the woods. The complete area would be searched thoroughly by the first daylight.

"Nothing from the tip line yet?" she asked.

Chomsky shook her head. "We're making progress," she said. "That's what matters. We'll find those children."

This had to weigh heavily on her, and not just because of the job. Luce knew that her boss had become a grandmother for the first time last year.

Everyone was worried about possible worst-case scenarios. What did the kidnappers want with these children? Why this particular bus, from this school?

"None of the parents have been contacted by the kidnappers?"

At this point, given the extent of this operation, they were almost certain that they were dealing with more than one perpetrator. The man who pretended to be Frank Reilly. Maybe even Frank Reilly himself. Potentially, someone else at the company.

Matt Layne? He was popular with the kids and the parents, but that didn't mean anything. He could be an excellent actor.

Those families all had one thing in common: Like Sarah Burke, they were affluent. Parents of kids in the same class. That was all.

"No," Chomsky confirmed.

"All right. I'll just make sure someone calls me in case they find anything."

"You do that. I'll see you in a few hours. Get some rest."

"I will."

Yet, when Luce stood at her desk, the idea of sleep made her feel too guilty. She sat down and opened up a file with notes she had taken during the interviews. There wasn't much.

Apparently, all the children were well behaved, nothing of the kind had ever happened.

They didn't have much time to talk to Matt Layne, but he had agreed to come to the station later today. As Luce had predicted, he had no problem with them showing up at his door, and he appeared genuinely scared for the children's safety.

As it was, he didn't know anything about a Frank Reilly.

"I wish I could help you," he'd said, looking every bit like someone who was suffering flu-like symptoms like he claimed. "It started all of a sudden on Sunday night. There was no way I could make it to work."

Impeccable timing. How had they pulled that off?

She didn't want to scare him, but she had suggested he'd go to the emergency room and have some tests done to be on the safe side.

Meanwhile, Ritter had spoken to Amelia Beckett, Principal Steyer's friend at the bus company, but she didn't know the real Frank Reilly well, wasn't aware of any complaints against him. She didn't know where he was staying either, though she had provided them with a couple of social media accounts of his. Another lead to follow. He hadn't posted anything about his vacation yet. Suspicious?

"Luce."

She turned around to see Tyler standing behind her.

"I'll be just a few more minutes," she said, feeling caught.

"No problem. You want to order something in?"

"No thanks. You go home. I will too. Soon."

"All right then. See you tomorrow—well, later today."

When he was gone, Luce headed to the break room to get a coffee from the vending machine. At her desk, she opened the drawer again and took out a bag of chips and a chocolate bar. It wasn't the romantic dinner that might have been on the table at some point, but it was enough for the guilt.

Those children might be hungry right now.

⁂

She had been hungry too, that time. The thought sprang to mind unbidden when Luce lay in her bed a few hours later, feeling queasy. Truth be told, every thought about that time was unwelcome. She had become better at keeping them at bay, but the idea of these children possibly being held somewhere, their fate unknown like Sarah's and Poppy's, was tough on her carefully established boundaries.

She was still hungry, Luce realized, unnerved. She had to sleep, clear her head, start again with fresh eyes.

Sheer exhaustion made her slip into sleep eventually, one that was far from restful.

She dreamed about the woods, walking around that bus, examining the empty seats inside.

"You're never going to find them."

The voice behind her made her spin around.

"They get what they deserve...and so will you."

She recoiled from Jared Hyde's maniacal laughter, only to realize that the back of the bus was open, and she stepped into nothing.

Luce woke with her heart racing, the t-shirt she wore damp, clinging to her skin.

"For Pete's sake," she mumbled and got out of bed. Five a.m. No messages on her phone. She went to the bathroom to take a shower, having every intention to leave for the station after a quick coffee.

After getting dressed, she sat on her bed for a few seconds, then laid back down. She could afford a few minutes maybe...The next time it was the doorbell that woke her.

Luce raked a hand through her hair, scowled at her mirror image and decided it would have to be enough. At least she was already dressed. She regretted her negligence a little when she opened the door to Kendra who was holding up a couple of bags with a smile.

"I thought that evenings might be tough in the next few days, and I didn't want to wait that long to see you. I hope this is okay."

It was better than okay. Everything Luce made out to be so complicated, Kendra made better.

"You brought breakfast," she said.

Kendra leaned in to kiss her softly, a greeting that finally chased the last cobwebs from her mind. There was a day beyond this case. A day beyond the nightmares of a barren room. She indulged both of them, pulling her closer.

When they stepped back, Kendra laughed.

"And you seem happy I did."

"I am. I have a deep and passionate love for fresh bagels." For a few seconds, they held each other's gaze.

She was lucky, so much, that Kendra saw through her, and that she was patient. The joke was laden with a different meaning, none that they could explore at this moment. But there was something she could do.

"I'll make us some coffee. I don't have a lot of—"

"Time, I know. I get it. But you still have to eat."

Suppressing a shudder, Luce thought of yesterday's diet of mostly coffee, potato chips, and a donut somewhere in between.

"Thank you for making sure I do."

They went to the kitchen where she prepared the coffee, and Kendra, who knew her way around, set the table.

"The transformation has been amazing," she said, indicating Luce's almost finished renovation project, the open concept kitchen/living space. Another aspect of her life that had been stalling before Kendra came into it. She made Luce believe she could do anything, and sometimes, that was scary.

"It has been," she agreed, pushing the button on the coffeemaker. She took out a couple of plates for the food Kendra had brought. Fresh bagels indeed. Cottage cheese and fruit. Oh well. It was a whole lot better than the vending machine snacks she might have gone for otherwise—again. "I think I can tackle the upstairs now."

They sat at the table. She was aware of Kendra studying her. Many unspoken things were swirling between them. At some point, she had fantasized about asking her to move in. It was still just a fantasy. Luce didn't want to move too fast with something that had proven to be the most important relationship in her adult life. Another scary thing.

"What about you? Is everything okay? You said something about an emergency?"

She couldn't bring herself to talk about the missing children, not now, when her guard was still somewhat down.

"Unfortunately, it's bound to happen. Same old, some don't know their rights, or someone in their life prevents them from exercising them. Or they are scared of the protesters outside. But we were able to save the patient."

Between the two of them, that made her the more successful. She didn't envy Kendra who was a doctor in a women's health clinic. She somehow managed to do her job every day against the multiple obstacles thrown in her way, without getting jaded.

Luce sometimes thought she'd been born jaded. Kendra's outlook on life had always intrigued her, and not that long ago, it had been a lifeline.

"That's good."

"They said on the news you found the school bus. I understand you can't talk about it, but I think the parents are lucky it's you on the case. You never give up."

Yet I'm having breakfast with my girlfriend at the moment.
She cast a glance at her phone. Nothing yet.

"It's not about that. We have steps to follow...and we hope we get a lucky break. That's the pattern."

"And you're modest too."

"Now you're yanking my chain."

"A little," Kendra admitted, smiling as she sipped her coffee. "But I'm not entirely unselfish. I really hope you find them safe and sound." Her tone and expression were a lot more sober in an instant. "It's horrible. And we can't even say who would do something like this, because that would be naïve, because we know. That doesn't keep me from hoping that they'll be okay—or that I'll have you to myself for a weekend sometime in the near future."

"You have me now," Luce said.

"Don't tempt me..."

Kendra's insinuation fell a little flat when her phone vibrated on the table.

"Oh well. I think breakfast is over. I'll see you soon."

"Definitely." Luce got up to see her to the door, and Kendra left after a goodbye kiss that was a bit quicker than the one before, but nonetheless promising.

Luce went back into the kitchen to clean up. After brushing her teeth and her hair, she left for work, bracing herself for possibilities good and horrific. Everything was possible, all the time.

Chapter Five

A s expected, their colleagues in the lab were still busy analyzing the evidence gathered at Frank Reilly's apartment,
and the scene in the woods. No sign of the children yet.

To no one's surprise, there were multiple prints on the bus.
Right now, they were focusing on the area around the driver's
seat.

Luce checked the real Frank Reilly's social media again. Still
no posts, and they still didn't know where exactly he was staying, not even a definite location. They had been checking out-
going flights, nothing so far. Caribbean, Beckett had said.

She did the same for Matt Layne who was easier to find. He
didn't have a lot of posts, but as she clicked through, she found
him tagged in a few pictures friends had taken, a barbecue, a
game.

And then her jaw dropped.

"Ritter, come here for a second."

He obliged without asking, the mix of disbelief and excitement in her tone apparently enough to make him curious. They
had replaced a tired nightshift earlier, but none of them had
gotten much sleep either.

This was...something.

"I'll be damned," he said when Luce pointed to the photo.
"He could still be in on it."

"Or someone wants to frame him," Luce reminded him.

"When did you become so generous?"

She ignored the comment. "This could be our lucky break. He could give us something on Brock—or vice versa."

"Not that generous then. Your bet is on the rich guy as usual."

"Not funny, Ritter. He's coming in half an hour from now—I guess we have a few questions we can add."

As if on cue, her phone rang, the officer on the front desk alerting her to Layne's arrival.

"And here he is."

Luce cast another glance at the photo, a smiling Matt Layne, his arm around Sarah Burke, Poppy Burke standing between them. They looked like one happy family. Were they?

She was going to find out.

Matt Layne still looked shaken when Luce and Ritter greeted him in the waiting area.

"Please tell me you have any idea where the children are," he said without preamble. "I'll tell you everything I know, but I'm afraid it's not much."

"We are getting closer," Ritter said vaguely. "Would you like a coffee? Luce?"

"Yes, thank you," she and Layne answered almost in unison. It had likely been a short night for both of them. Had guilt kept him up too or was he worried sick about Sarah and Poppy?

They settled in an interrogation room where Luce shuffled some papers until Ritter arrived with three coffees.

"Okay, Mr. Layne, thank you for coming in. How did it go at the hospital?"

"They said it could have been food poisoning," he said with a shrug. "It wasn't conclusive. But I'm fine now, so I guess no one was trying to kill me." He laughed uneasily. "That's good news, right?"

"Indeed. I'd like us to go over this one more time—from the moment you called in sick."

"Yeah. It's strange, like I told you yesterday, it started on Sunday all of a sudden. Must have been some sort of stomach flu. Don't worry, I don't think it's contagious. Strange, I haven't been sick like this in years. Anyway, I called the office, and they usually send a replacement."

"Mr. Frank Reilly."

"I assume. Like I told you, I never met him. They have people from all over the county working for them, and we're not always there at the same time. Comes with the territory."

"And you have no idea who could have an interest in abducting these children?"

"What? Of course not! I love my job. The parents know they can rely on me. I hate that this is happening, but you can't blame me for—"

"We are not blaming you for anything," she interrupted him. At least not yet. "We just have to make sure we haven't missed any details. So, you're familiar with most of the parents, I guess."

"That depends. I know their names, and the kids can be chatty sometimes. That's it."

"It's a wealthy neighborhood."

"True. That's probably why they took them? You received a ransom yet?"

"Mr. Layne, how well do you know Sarah Burke?"

He sat back, his expression carefully neutral.

"She's the mom of one of the missing kids."

"I got the feeling she might be more to you than that."

Layne shook his head. "I don't know what you're talking about."

"You take pictures like that with all the moms?"

His eyes widened when she showed him the photo she'd printed out earlier, and he cursed. Luce exchanged a glance with Ritter.

"You are not exactly an open book on social media, but some of your friends are. A dozen kids from the bus you usually drive are missing, and so is your girlfriend, Sarah Burke. Matt, I think you owe us an explanation."

"It's not what you think." He wiped a hand over his face, clearly upset. "When I couldn't reach Sarah, I thought she was trying to lay low. That photo should never have been online. Is it true? Was Poppy on that bus? Oh my God. This is just getting worse."

Luce took a moment to absorb what he'd said and determine how much of it she was willing to believe.

"If you thought she wasn't, why didn't you tell me and my colleague yesterday?"

And how could you know if you weren't involved in either abduction?

"I'm sorry. It was late, I'd been sleeping for the better part of two days, and...it's all pretty confusing. I was really hoping Sarah had just gone into hiding, and that he didn't come after her." This time, he held Luce's gaze. "All right, yes, we are together, but she preferred to keep it under wraps for now. Her ex is a vengeful asshole, and she didn't want him to know that we were dating."

"That must have been pretty frustrating," Ritter remarked. "Especially when she's still somewhat financially depending on him."

"Wait, what, did he tell you that? Yes, the guy is loaded, but Sarah wasn't poor when she met him. She has a pretty good job and had inherited some money of her own. That's how she was able to have a home in that neighborhood and send Poppy to Carter Academy."

Was either man unhappy with those facts? Luce wouldn't be surprised. The rich husband who couldn't impress with his wealth, because the woman had some of her own. The younger boyfriend in a different salary bracket, trying to keep up.

"All right. Tell me a bit more about Sarah. Did you ever have the impression that she was struggling?"

"With what? Oh, you mean, other than her ex being an asshole to her? She overlooks a lot because of Poppy, but I know it was starting to get to her. Sarah is an amazing woman, and mother. If he told you otherwise, he's lying. He's been trying to get her back ever since the divorce, even though he cheated on her. Imagine."

He was obviously passionate about Sarah. That could mean many things.

Luce's instincts told her that Brock wanted to paint a certain picture of his ex-wife, though Matt might be doing the same about the ex-husband to distract from himself. There were still too many options for her liking.

"In your opinion, would he use violence to get her back?"

He shrugged. "Everything is possible. I don't know if that's what happened, but I'm sure he's capable."

"And Sarah, did she ever mention that getting back together with him was a possibility?"

"No! We are planning to get married."

"Okay. You said she might have gone into hiding. How long have you been making those marriage plans? Could he have found out?"

"I don't know." He cast another glance at Luce's phone. "She wasn't tagged in the picture, so if he was looking for her, he wouldn't have found her. She, we were very careful, usually."

The phone on the wall rang, and Ritter got up to get it.

He listened for a moment, then said, "I understand," before he hung up. "We have to end this here, Mr. Layne. If there's anything else you can think of, please let us know. Allen?"

Still, too many possibilities. It came down to who had the most resources to make a dozen children disappear on their way home from school—and who had the most interest in making Sarah Burke disappear at the same time.

Brock still looked good to Luce though she couldn't help thinking that there was more to Layne's story than he had shared.

"Thank you," she said. "We'll be in touch."

⁓

They met in the conference room with Lieutenant Chomsky, Tyler and two other detectives on the school bus case. Luce noticed that D.A. Troy was present as well. She sat at the end of the table frowning at an open file.

Her demeanor couldn't have been more different to Carrie Brayden's. The head lab technician came rushing in, carrying files and a laptop.

"Okay, you'll like this," she said. "You can imagine we've been a bit overwhelmed with all the evidence that has come in from the two scenes, but we have something. The apartment was wiped down reasonably well, but we still got some DNA and prints. The former will take a little longer, but the prints were the same as some that we've found in the bus."

"Frank Reilly," Luce said.

"Yes, and no." She opened up a file and showed it to them. "This is Frank Reilly's picture on the file the school had on him, the guy who's conveniently out of the country. This is the man who drove the bus and spent some time in the apartment." She laid a mug shot next to the other paper. "Voilà. Adam Wheeler. Served for assault and robbery, got out on probation last year."

"How does a man like that get to drive a bus with 3rd graders?"

For once, Luce could agree with every emotion audible in Troy's tone. She and the D.A. had their disagreements—this wasn't one of them.

"Apparently the school didn't suspect anything. They got the paperwork they usually get from the company," Luce explained. "They, however, say they never got a request or sent anyone."

"Find out if there's anybody at the company who helped him," Chomsky said. "Priority is to find this man."

Luce agreed with that too. The many theories in her head could wait for a bit, as long as they found Wheeler, and with him, the children first.

She had to confirm though.

"What are we going to do about Brock? Mr. Layne made some pretty hefty accusations against him."

"We're talking about Brock Constructions, right? His ex-wife is missing?" Troy verified. "It looks like Layne has some things to hide as well."

Why would that make a difference? Luce decided there was no time get into this with the D.A. She was confident that finding the missing children would eventually lead them to Sarah and Poppy as well.

"Possibly," she ascertained. "Okay, let's get rolling on Wheeler. I'm sure he has some answers for us."

❦

They obtained a last known address from Wheeler's parole officer.

"He's doing everything he's supposed to do," the man told Luce over the phone. "Is he just going through the motions? Maybe, but there hasn't been anything to report. Can I ask what this is about?"

"Mr. Wheeler is a person of interest at this point," she told him. "Thank you for your time."

She hung up and picked up the address she had jotted down on her notepad.

"We can check with the bus company on the way."

"I can come with you," Tyler offered.

"I meant Ritter and I," she said. "I'd prefer if you stayed here and let us know as soon as you learn anything new. Also, the information on Wheeler needs to go out to every squad car. We found the bus, we will find those children. See if you can turn up anything else on him, anything that might help us figure out what his role is in this. I might be wrong, but he doesn't look like the mastermind to me."

"Yes, Ma'am." Much to his credit, it didn't sound the least bit ironic.

Luce and Ritter left for Wheeler's address. As excited as she was about the progress, she couldn't help wondering if they'd find anything of importance in the place. The fact that they even had those prints—sloppiness on someone's part, or a distraction?

They came up to an old, otherwise non-descript building in an area far from the pristine front lawns of Sarah Burke's neighborhood.

"What's your take on Layne?" she asked. "You think he's telling the truth about Brock?"

"I don't know. In any case, it sounds similar to what the housekeeper told you. It's pretty clear that there was an abuser in Sarah's life, and it might be Brock."

She could tell he was hesitating. "Layne? I can't imagine that. He might be a good actor, but how would he pull off all of this? He never even saw Wheeler. The parents have known him for a long time. I'm sure we would have learned by now if there were any problems."

"You know that for certain? A lot of predators hide in plain sight."

The thought made her sick to her stomach. For the children. For the memory still swirling in her mind. To her, Hyde had been so obvious. It had been a source of frustration for her that so few people could see the danger coming from individuals like him.

She didn't get the same vibe from Layne. He seemed seriously upset about the fact that the picture with him and Sarah had made its way onto social media. But what if he was hiding something else?"

As if reading her thoughts, Ritter continued, "I guess we can agree that those children going missing on the same day as Burke and her daughter is not a coincidence. But we don't know yet which one is the real target, and which one the distraction."

"True."

"What if Sarah and Poppy did leave of their own volition?" Ritter mused out loud.

"You think Matt Layne is trying to set up Brock? That they faked the abduction?"

"It's a theory. Think about it. There was no violence that we could tell."

Luce wasn't convinced. "Brock could have threatened them with a gun. Sarah wouldn't risk her daughter's life."

"Fair enough, but...I'm not saying Brock isn't a bad guy. Maybe he found out about their relationship, made threats about custody or even to Sarah's life..."

"So, Matt hires an ex-con to abduct the kids from his bus, so we'll be busy, while...what? It didn't look like he was about to go into hiding."

"It could have been the plan, and they had to pivot? Just keep it in mind," Ritter advised. "Now, let's see what we can learn here."

The super gave them the key without asking any questions once they identified themselves. "Fifth floor, Apartment 503," he grumbled and went back to whatever he was watching on his laptop. Luce wasn't sure she wanted to know.

"Thank you, sir."

He grunted something in her direction, and then, she and Ritter were on their way.

Outdated wallpaper was peeling from the wall, the carpet in the hall an uninspired brown. When they came up to the door, one of the numbers was upside down, but what was more concerning was the fact that the door wasn't locked.

"Shit," Luce mumbled, carefully turning the knob with a gloved hand.

"Mr. Wheeler?" she called. "Police. We're coming in. We need to talk to you."

Silence greeted them.

There was silence, and then there was...This, Luce reflected, a heavy atmosphere reeking of doom. They examined the tiny apartment, a small closed-off living room, a bathroom to the side, and the bedroom. On the floor, a man lay sprawled on his back. The front of his shirt was soaked in blood.

Luce recognized Adam Wheeler as she knelt next to him to check for a pulse. She could barely feel one.

"He's alive, but not for much longer. We need to get an ambulance in here."

Her vision danced in front of her for a second, and she could tell from Ritter's expression that he had to be thinking of the same thing. A second later he was on the phone calling an ambulance, and he hurried to get a towel from the bathroom to stop the flow from the still bleeding wound.

"Don't you fucking die on me," Luce whispered as she pressed down. If they lost him, they'd lose their best chance to bring the missing kids home.

Chapter Six

They searched the apartment with a couple of uniformed officers while Wheeler was rushed to the hospital. Luce and Ritter worked quietly side by side. They weren't fooling themselves. There was a good chance that Wheeler would never wake up.

That made it even more important for them not to overlook the smallest detail.

They opened cabinets, drawers, a microwave that looked like it hadn't been cleaned since its last use a while ago. The space was limited—even "Frank Reilly's" place seemed bigger in her memory, but that might be because it had barely any furniture in it.

Luce's frustration rose the closer they came to the end of the search. He had left the map in the other apartment, but not much else. If he had felt safe here, there had to be some sort of communication device. She reasoned that whoever had shot him had probably taken any phone or laptop in his possession. Given Wheeler's background, they might be looking at an unrelated event, though she didn't think that was the case.

The disappearance of Sarah Burke and her daughter, the children on the bus, this man, everything had happened in too quick succession not to be related.

She caught her breath for a second, unable to push away the dire thoughts any longer. If there was no ransom, it meant that whoever had taken the children had no intention of returning them or even keeping up appearances. Human trafficking came to mind.

What made Kendra good at her job, and in life, was that she believed that enough good people existed alongside evil ones.

Luce, on the other hand, held on to her disgust in humanity. She was rarely surprised.

"There's nothing here," Ritter commented. "Not even a cable."

"He didn't think they were coming after him, so he didn't consider any sort of insurance," she mused out loud. "I don't know. He probably never imagined he might end up being the fall guy. Did he try to negotiate more than his share?"

"A loose end. Sometimes it's as easy as that."

Easy was not a word Luce would use to describe the situation, but she couldn't deny he had a point.

"Let's go over the place one more time."

"What are you trying to find?" There was a small hint of irritation to his tone. "We've been over every square inch. There's nothing here."

"I don't know." She didn't, but something made her want to stay. Desperation, most likely. She didn't want to bring bad news to the parents. Luce hadn't had time to look at the headlines much, but the press coverage ranged from praising the hard-working cops on the case to damning them for not making any progress.

"We still have to drop by the bus company."

"I'm aware. Give me a few more minutes."

Once again, she went from room to room. *Think!* The perpetrator had shot Wheeler point blank, and given that the lock looked undisturbed, he either had a key, or Wheeler had let him in. An accomplice?

Ritter's expression didn't hide his frustration, but he followed her without further comment when she went back into the claustrophobic bathroom and examined the shower, each cabinet, the space under the sink. In the bedroom, she lifted the mattress once more, looked under the bed.

"Luce."

She picked up the lamp on the nightstand, surprised by how heavy it was.

"No," he said in disbelief when she shook it, and a sound indicated something inside the ceramic cylinder. "I'll be damned."

Luce turned it over and tried to reach inside, but the opening was too small. She didn't waste any time and smashed it onto the floor instead.

A sim card, wrapped in plastic, was inside, along with a burner phone and a charger.

"He had insurance after all. Smart guy," she said. "There should be something on this for us."

※

In the officers' squad car, they managed to get a first look at the files on the sim card. Luce barely kept herself from showing her enthusiasm by letting out an undignified squeal. She didn't do that, ever, especially not in front of colleagues, but she came close enough when they got to see the contents of the card—not encrypted. Either Wheeler had used this as blackmail material, or he wanted to world to know details in case something happened to him.

This would help with a solid conviction.

One of the folders held details about the route and schedule of the school bus. Another looked like someone had done meticulous surveillance on Matt Layne. One of the blurrier pictures showed him at a park with a dark-haired woman and a child: Sarah and Poppy.

So, Wheeler had to be involved in their disappearance, the photo linking the two cases together.

"We'll keep that in mind," Luce said. "Next, tell us where those children are, damn it."

Another folder was filled with pictures of what looked like construction sites, houses in various stages of completion. Luce remembered the company they'd passed on the way to where they had found the location of the bus.

She looked through all of them, until she found one that showed a part of the company's placard.

"Look at this. That's one of Brock's sites. We have to find out where this is, and we have to bring him in."

"I agree with you on the former. The latter, I'm not sure Troy will go for it."

"I don't care! We don't need her for this, anyway. I'm not planning to arrest him, just have a friendly chat over at the station for now. Let's go. The bus company can wait for a moment."

To the officers, she said, "Get this right to the lab, and have them call me if there's anything regarding the location of either the bus, or Sarah and Poppy Burke. Thanks."

Ritter didn't argue, and they went back to their own vehicle to get to Brock's office.

Brock was not amused to be called out of a meeting, and he made his displeasure clear.

"Detectives, you again? Shouldn't you be out there looking for Poppy...and those other kids?"

"I'm very sorry for the inconvenience," Luce told him. She was still coasting on the excitement of strands about to unravel, unfazed by his attitude. It might change soon once he realized why they had sought him out again. "We have to know if you recognize this. It's important."

"Of course I do. It's one of our sites. It's a hotel that will be open in the fall. What does that have to do with anything?"

"There are a few others here. I need you to go over them and give me the addresses of each location you recognize." On second thought, she asked, "Is this the one closest to being finished?"

"Let me look. Yes, this one is close to being finished. We had to take a break because of an environmental issue." He frowned. "What are you saying? You don't think—"

"I need those addresses, now."

Fortunately, he seemed to understand that this wasn't the time to stall. With the information on hand, they jogged back to the car and got in.

They used the siren on the way, once again sharing hope and silence. It was a start, but they might have to go over more sites. They might be wrong after all.

Luce and Ritter didn't talk about what they might find. In fact, the only words spoken on the way were during a call for backup. The hotel was going to be a vast complex.

As Brock had said, the place was close to being finished. From the looks of it, only smaller details were still missing.

Did the place have heat and water? Luce wondered. She had done searches in strange places, often under pressure. Not so long ago, she had woken up in one. And another time, her partner had been shot.

It was enough to nearly bring on a flashback, make her heart pound. Backup had arrived, several officers assisting them as they went through the unfinished rooms. She could see where the gym would be, the pool, offices, and a lounge area. In the restaurant/bar space, a spiral staircase led upstairs to another huge space with multiple hallways and doors. She assumed that this was where bedrooms would be. She could hear the muted voices of her colleagues walking overhead. More space. More doors. This was a giant complex.

Whatever Brock had done, or not done, it wasn't a secret that he was, as Matt Layne had put it, loaded. It made no sense that someone would abduct his ex-wife and child without asking for money...unless...

That's when she heard the sound, someone crying in utter distress. A child.

Luce ran the last steps to the door where the sound seemed to be coming from. Unlike others on this floor, it was locked.

"Hello?" she called. "The police are here. We're going to get you out." The crying quieted. She was in equal parts excited and scared about what she was going to find on the other side.

"Are you really the police?" a small voice asked, sounding doubtful.

"I am. My name is Luce."

She thought she might have to kick the door, but to her relief, she found a screwdriver nearby. No need to make a mess.

"Hang in there," she called. "Almost there."

"What are you—my God."

Luce didn't take the time to turn around and face Ritter. She kept working, a few minutes until the screws finally moved and the lock fell.

Her hand trembled when she opened the door, which might have been from gripping the screwdriver so tightly, or sheer anxiety.

The image was momentarily overlaid by that of a group of scared teenage girls, then she told herself to get a grip—and counted the children huddled in the corner, looking at her through frightened eyes. Twelve children. All of the missing ones from the bus, accounted for, except for Poppy Burke, but she had expected that.

"Okay, let's get them checked out at the hospital, and call the parents," she said, pushing back the emotions that threatened her composure. This was close to a happy ending, but they weren't there yet.

She carefully approached the group, noticing that there was another door. A bathroom, she hoped. There was a huge fridge and a shelf holding cereal boxes and other food, and some plastic dishes. Relief changed into a familiar anger, but she didn't have time for either.

"Is anyone of you hurt?" she asked. Priorities.

All of the children had cried at some point, easy to see from the streaks on their faces. Most of them looked alert and physically unharmed, though she could see that one of the girls had a small bruise on the side of her face.

"One of the bad guys hit Caitlyn because she bit him," one of the boys said. Luce recognized the light blonde hair of Justin Dennis. He seemed to feel the same anger as she did.

"We will get all of you checked out at the hospital, we'll have a few questions, and then your parents will take you home," she promised. "You're Caitlyn?"

The girl nodded.

"You are safe now. You all are."

She could hear the sirens, grateful that their ordeal was about to come to an end. She wasn't looking forward to those questions she would have to ask. She had hated answering them, and she wasn't a frightened eight-year-old.

Another one of the boys looked like he was barely awake, which worried her. Had they been given drugs? The sooner they could figure it all out, the better.

A group of paramedics joined them and started to examine the children while Luce and Ritter went on to confirm identities.

On a hunch, she sat next to Justin.

"I'm sure this was extremely scary, but can you tell me what happened? We found the school bus."

"He stopped on the way," Justin said. "Matt always said you're not supposed to unless there's an emergency, but he just drove up to the woods and said he had a surprise, because it was his birthday."

"The man named Frank Reilly?"

"Yes. He had brownies for everyone."

That son of a b—Luce suppressed the thought. Her own feelings didn't matter. She sincerely hoped that Wheeler would wake up so he could be held accountable for his role in this mess.

"What happened next?"

"I didn't eat all of it. I noticed that the others fell asleep soon after, so I pretended to be too. But there was no chance to run away, and I didn't want to leave them alone."

"You are very brave, Justin." She lightly touched his shoulder and got to her feet when the paramedic approached them. "We'll talk some more later, okay?"

"Okay," he said, some of the bravado leaving him as realization that the nightmare was over, sank in. "Please take care of Caitlyn...and Tommy, he's been very sleepy ever since."

"Don't worry, we will."

Chapter Seven

L uce took a deep breath when the children were gone from the room. She made a quick call to Lieutenant Chomsky.

"Amazing news, Detective. We are in the process of notifying the parents."

"We'll meet them at the hospital," she confirmed. "Once we have their statements, I'd like to talk to Mr. Brock again."

"You do that. I want to know how those children ended up in his hotel complex."

So, she might test the waters with Troy. It was going to be a good day. Now, if only Caitlyn and Tommy were okay, too, and Wheeler recovered enough to talk...

Perfection.

The fact that this brought her closer to the planned dinner with Kendra didn't harm either.

The smile vanished from her face when she took a quick look around the surroundings the children had spent the past thirty-six hours in.

Someone had made sure they had food and water for at least a couple of days, but no beds, only a few chairs and cushions on the floor. The bathroom wasn't quite finished, and the smell made her recoil.

When she left the room, it was with the grim determination to hold everyone involved in this accountable. She was certain that Ritter felt the same.

❧

The media circus unfolding in front of the clinic did not come as a surprise. Hospital security was trying to secure the perimeter, a challenging job between the legitimate press and the growing crowd of bystanders, some happy, some...just weird.

"Did aliens abduct those kids?"

Luce didn't turn around, but she shared an incredulous look with Ritter. He shrugged.

"Told you so," he said.

They finally made it to the floor where the rescued children were being taken care of and reunited with their anxious but relieved parents. After identifying themselves to the nurse at the front desk, the first order of business was to find a doctor who could tell them about their condition.

On the way, Luce caught a glimpse behind a three quarters drawn curtain, a tearful hug.

"It's a good day," she said quietly.

"It's a Goddamn miracle," Ritter commented.

Same difference.

The doctor had more relieving news for them. "It seems like all of them were dosed with a sedative, but not enough to cause harm. One of them, Tommy Jensen, had a bit of a harder time shaking it, but his vitals look good. I understand that they had food and water." His face darkened. "For a few days."

"Whoever took them, locked them in with limited supplies and an out of order toilet. We were lucky we found them when we did." She wasn't asking for a psychiatric evaluation, and she didn't need one at the moment. Despite the clear upsides, this had been a traumatic experience. Those kids would have more to shake than the drug. "What about Caitlyn?"

"A superficial bruise. Nearly all of them have told me in admiring tones about how she bit that son of a—sorry."

"No need." After all, she had fought the same impulse, but swearing wouldn't change the facts. And neither of them was here to make themselves feel better.

"She'll be fine. They will all be, at least physically."

That was...something. A huge something. They would offer the parents a few contacts to help with the other part, but first they had to ask those questions.

"There you are. Hey. This is amazing."

She nearly thought Tyler Murphy was going to hug her. Even though that might have been awkward, she couldn't help smiling.

"It is," she agreed. "Chomsky sent you to help with the interviews?"

"Exactly. Where do we start?"

"I'd like to talk to Justin and Caitlyn last. I believe they might have the most to say. Justin wasn't as impacted by the drug as the others."

"All right. Chomsky told me all of the parents have arrived now, we better get started before they go home."

Four families for each of them.

When she walked into the first room, Luce held her head a bit higher than she had before.

"Good afternoon. My name is Detective Allen." She was going to launch into an apology for having to bother them after this horrific experience when the woman all but jumped up and wrapped her arms around Luce.

She was getting hugged after all.

Caitlyn was the third child on her list. Her two moms were sitting on either side of her bed, one of them getting up to greet Luce in a calmer fashion.

"Detective, thank you. I know you have to do this, but please, be careful, okay?"

The girl made a sound suspiciously close to a snort. Given everything she knew about her, Luce really liked her already, even though she understood her actions could have come at a higher cost. Being someone who talked back to bullies and had faced the consequences, she could relate.

"I promise you, we'll do this as quickly as possible. Hi again, Caitlyn. I'd just like you to tell me in your own words what you remember."

"Didn't you ask the others already?"

"Yes, we did. But you know, people remember different details sometimes, and everything is important. We want to find who did this to you."

"He said his name was Frank, and he was driving because Matt was sick," she recalled. "He gave us brownies, because it was his birthday." She sighed. "That was a lie."

"I think so too. You fell asleep?"

"Yes, and when I woke up, we were in the back of a car. A truck."

"Like this box truck?"

Luce showed her a picture, a stock photo that closest fit the description the others had given.

"Yes. It was very shaky." Her eyes were starting to well up, and her mothers instinctively leaned closer.

"I can imagine. That must have been scary, but you all made it."

"It was dark when we got there. They locked us in, and that's where I thought..." She shook her head. "It was stupid."

"No. You were trying to do something. I understand. You said they?"

"Frank, and another man. They left us there. Tommy was still asleep, they just dragged him in there. It made me mad."

"That I understand too. We know what Frank looks like, but can you tell us anything about the other man?"

Caitlyn shrugged. "He had a beard. Jeans and a T-shirt, and he smelled funny. He was the one who hit me."

Luce hated to make her cry, but there was no way she could stop, not for another few minutes.

"You've ever smelled that smell before?"

"Yes, no...I don't know."

"That's all right. You did great, Caitlyn. You all did. We'll have to check a few things right now, but we might have a few more questions. Those can wait until later though."

When she was about to leave, one of the women held her back.

"Can I ask what you're doing to find these men?"

Her mixed emotions came across clearly.

Luce cast a look over her shoulder, but none of her colleagues were anywhere to be seen. She hadn't heard the question for the first time either, and she was tired of giving a standard answer.

"Everything we can. The one they describe as Frank is currently being treated for a gunshot wound. We don't know yet if he's going to make it, but there's still some evidence to go through. I promise you we will hold them accountable."

She could tell that her words had an impact.

"Thank you. If you'll excuse me now...We have to talk to the other parents. We'll be in touch if there's anything else."

The woman nodded. "Just let us know when you found them."

Next was Justin Dennis and his parents. The latter were proud to share that he and Caitlyn had taken on the job of the adults during their ordeal, calming everyone, distributing food, trying to help them through the ordeal best they could.

She wondered how Murphy and Ritter were doing. So far, this had gone so much better than expected.

"Have you found Poppy too?" he asked at the end of the interview, startling her.

"Poppy Burke is in your class, right? But she wasn't in the bus with you that day."

Poppy and Sarah had gone missing before the other children did. How could he even know about that?

"We saw something on TV earlier," his father explained. "He might be confusing something."

"I am not." Justin was indignant. "I saw her."

"Honey, you're tired. How about we get out of here and get something to eat?" Leona Dennis pleaded. "Anything you like."

That was almost amusing. Luce was certain that similar offers were on the table for all the children, and she wondered what their choices would be. She of all people could understand the urge to indulge oneself after beating the odds.

"I'll let you be in a few minutes," Luce promised. "Justin, did you see Poppy on TV?"

"Yes, of course."

"We are looking for her and her mom. I promise you."

"Not just on TV. On Frank's phone."

The blurry picture in the folder on the memory card came to mind.

"When did you see that?"

"Monday, on the bus. I think he didn't want me to see it because he turned it off right away." His eyes widened. "I should have told right away."

"You couldn't know," Luce assured him. "This is not your fault, you hear me?"

He nodded, still clearly shaken.

"Okay. Thank you so much, Justin. That was very helpful."

She almost wished someone would offer *her* a dinner of anything she liked, but she'd have to wait a few more hours for that. Or hit the vending machine again.

Chapter Eight

L uce had time for half a coffee and a chocolate bar before she and Tyler went into the room with Brock who had grudgingly agreed to come in and talk to them. She thought ruefully that as long as she was "indulging," she should be upgrading to better snacks and caffeine fixes. Tonight should be better. She might cook a real meal—or at least order one.

First things first.

She and Tyler stood in the observation area, watching Brock giving his watch an impatient look.

"He doesn't miss any opportunity to tell us how busy he is. What I want to know is how he could not know that someone was hiding a bunch of kidnapped children on a site still in progress."

"Let's ask him," Tyler said, and they went into the room.

Luce remained standing to the side while Tyler sat across from Brock.

"I hope you have an update on where Sarah took my daughter. I'm beginning to think I need to employ some of my own resources. My in-house investigator might do a better job."

Tyler took the accusation in stride while Luce watched, hoping to find the man blink. They already knew Wheeler and another man yet unknown were involved. There was no way Matt Layne could have hired them, then either sent a hitman to

Wheeler's apartment, or done the job himself. It all seemed too elaborate for the jealous boyfriend, or the protective boyfriend. He just didn't have the means. Brock did.

Suppressing a sigh, Luce had to admit she couldn't rule out completely that he simply reminded her of another wealthy man whose privilege had turned to crime.

She wished it wasn't true. But what was the alternative?

"Thanks to the information you gave my colleagues earlier, they could locate and return the missing children. We appreciate your help," Tyler stated.

"Well, yeah. That doesn't bring Poppy back, does it?"

"I can assure you we are working on that, but this is important too. Has an Adam Wheeler ever worked on one of those sites?"

"I would have to check. I have hundreds of people working on those sites, and as you can imagine, I don't deal with each of them individually. You'd have to ask the foremen and the project managers. The name doesn't ring a bell if that's what you mean."

"Okay. Frank Reilly?"

"No. Not that I'm aware of."

"So, you've never met either of those men?"

They had a photo for Wheeler, and a sketch for the second man. Brock studied both and shook his head.

"I don't know what that has to do with anything, but no. I have no idea who they are."

Luce had the strangest feeling that he was telling the truth. There went her theory.

"Mr. Brock," she said, "do you have any idea why they would choose the hotel complex to hide the children?" She could tell that he was struggling to hold back an angry answer. "Look, if one of them was a disgruntled employee, they might do this as a way to get back at you. If anything, it will disrupt the progress as the site is now a crime scene."

"It's inconvenient, true, but it's by far not our only project. The rest is just...fiction. We've had employees leaving, but no one as crazy as you describe."

"We understand," Tyler kept his tone conversational. "What about Matt Layne? What can you tell us about him?"

"That school bus driver? Hotheaded young man. I didn't think he should be driving children around. He threatened me once. I complained to the school, but obviously they didn't do anything about it."

"Why did he threaten you?" Luce prompted, doubtful. He was losing her again. His story seemed manufactured, just like Sarah's "issues."

"You'd have to ask him. He freaked out because I was talking to my wife. I told him off. It nearly got physical, but I think he realized that I could afford the better lawyers."

It was interesting that Layne hadn't mentioned the argument. They'd have to get back to that too.

"Is that all? I need to get back to the office."

"Of course. I'll see you out," Tyler offered.

Alone in the room, Luce thought about how Brock never once asked about the children's condition. Almost like he couldn't care less.

☙

The atmosphere in the room was tangibly lighter when Luce started to work on her report. Many of her colleagues were still busy analyzing the files from the card Wheeler had hidden, but so far, the contents mostly related to the planning of the abduction—including the file on Matt Layne.

Wheeler didn't seem to have paid much attention to his relationship with Sarah, though she was certain that Brock had known. He still called her his wife. Justin had seen her on Wheeler's phone.

Something didn't add up. As daylight started to fade outside, Luce was starting to resign to the fact that she wasn't going to figure it out today. She hoped that wherever Sarah and Poppy were, their circumstances were better than the ones the children had been in.

"Hey, Luce."

She looked up at Tyler who had walked up to her desk.

"Care to join us for a few drinks tonight?" She saw that Ritter and Meyers were also finishing up.

It was on the tip of her tongue to say no, for several reasons. She hadn't been out with colleagues for some time, mostly because she rarely drank. Of course, Tyler wouldn't know that about her, because on the few occasions they'd hung out before, she had had a few drinks.

For other reasons too—but she knew as well as they all did that today could have gone various ways. None of the kids had reported assault other than what happened to Caitlyn—which was bad enough, and at the same time, by far not the worst she and each of her colleagues had ever dealt with. There was something to be said about marking those moments.

"Where are we going?" she asked. "I'd just like to make a call first. Two, actually."

"No problem. We can catch up later. How about the bar at the end of the block, Mike's Corner?"

"I'll be there."

Her first call was to the hospital only to learn that Wheeler hadn't woken up yet.

The second went to Kendra.

"Luce! I'm happy you called."

She sounded happy. Luce could feel the day, the worries, the worst-case scenarios, release her from its clutches.

"You found the children. It's amazing! The parents must be so relieved."

"They are, and it wasn't just me," Luce reasoned. "Where are you?"

"I'm about to head home. Would you like to come over?"

"I was wondering if you wanted to join me...us. A few colleagues and I are getting drinks."

"Oh. At a cop bar." Kendra sounded both hesitant and intrigued. "You should celebrate, but are you sure you want me—"

"Yes. Please. It's not celebrating. Just to unwind for a bit."

"All right. I can use that too. I'll be there."

Now Luce was happy too.

"I'll text you the address. Can't wait to see you."

When she ended the call, she realized that Tyler had never left. She wondered how much he had overheard.

"You're ready?" he asked.

"Ready. Let's go."

It wasn't until they had left the building that she realized he had meant that literally, but she figured she could either come back to get her car tonight or do it tomorrow.

"I know what you're thinking," he said when they walked down the street.

"No, you don't. I am so glad these kids are back home. I wish the same could be true for Sarah and Poppy, but I'm realistic. The nightshift is on the lookout. We'll pick it up tomorrow. That's all we can do."

It was almost comical to think she'd made him speechless.

"You got me there," he admitted. "But I'm glad you came to that conclusion. A while ago, things were a lot more tense, for a reason. I get that."

"It's okay. We don't need to talk it through."

"I wasn't going to...Okay." He laughed a little. "You're still seeing the doctor, right? For what it's worth, I think you are good together."

Not like she needed his permission, but she knew him well enough to understand how he meant it, so Luce let it slide.

"I happen to think so too," she said.

Kendra might think of her request as strange since so far, their circles of friends hadn't overlapped much. Not that Luce had many friends. She assumed that Kendra's outlook on life lent itself more to making them, even though she, too, didn't socialize a lot outside of work.

After focusing on the job, giving it the best you could, there was only so much of a reminder you could tolerate. At least that had been Luce's reasoning so far.

When they walked over the threshold and into the crowded bar, the relief at knowing she would join her, helped release some of the tension from her shoulders.

The fact that she had even been worried for a minute, frustrated her. It had nothing to do with anything. She could have a beer after work. It meant normalcy.

Ritter and Meyers occupied a table in the back where Luce and Tyler joined them. Even though the place was packed, a popular hangout for employees of companies in the area, the music wasn't too loud. Luce had been here a couple of times and found the food to be surprisingly good. She might even go for the special—healthy cooking could wait another day.

She had decided she didn't want to question every good thing in her life any longer. In the beginning, Luce had worried how adding Tyler to the unit might change the dynamics, but he seemed to be at ease, and so were their other colleagues.

She talked to Jill more often these days, and there was a deeper understanding between them.

And...

"There you are." Kendra leaned in for a quick, almost unreal kiss. Ritter pulled a chair for her, and she sat next to Luce. It wasn't a dramatic public display of affection, just...comfortingly normal. The ground didn't open up. Perhaps, this whole time, Luce had been the only dramatic one.

"Hey," she said, feeling a goofy smile spread over her face. She had it bad, no doubt about it. "You all know Kendra."

They did indeed, had met her a few months ago when Lieutenant Chomsky had asked her to come in as a witness, when Luce was missing.

No big deal. Except it was.

"Now we got that out of the way, how about we get some food on the table?" Meyers suggested.

"I thought you'd never ask," she returned.

Kendra smiling at her made her blush. It was all part of the new and exciting life.

Chapter Nine

The food had indeed been fantastic. Since Luce had let herself be talked into a second round—not Kendra's fault—she had decided to take a cab she shared with Kendra. In the back, they kissed some more.

Luce was pretty sure she had never felt like this, or at least not in a long time. Allowing herself to take a break from the demands of not only her job, but her own expectations, spend time with her colleagues and the woman she had fallen in love with...It all made sense now. It all fit together. She didn't need to know more.

"Come home with me?" She whispered, because she was aware of the driver already trying hard to keep a straight face. She didn't usually do things like this, make out in the back of a taxi. Maybe Kendra didn't, either. This had to mean something.

Kendra leaned into her with a happy sigh, but her words were less encouraging.

"I'd love to, but I have a meeting first thing in the morning, and patients non-stop. To be honest, I shouldn't have even come tonight, but I know today was a big win for you. That, and I really wanted to see you."

"Seeing me doesn't seem to be the problem." Luce leaned back in her seat.

"What does that mean?" Kendra asked calmly. Her tone was void of judgment, yet Luce couldn't help feeling the atmosphere had changed. Was it just her? Usually, it was her.

"I'm not sure. This has been going on for weeks. We see each other, but there's always something getting in the way. I thought you wanted to move forward with this...Us."

"I want that very much." Kendra too, was whispering.

Luce found nothing but sincerity in her gaze and voice, and she couldn't deal with any of it.

"Do *you*?" Kendra asked softly.

"Of course." There was no question, none whatsoever. And she had something else to address. "You know you don't have to walk on eggshells around me. Everything that happened, with Hyde, yes, it really sucked, but it's over. I'm over it. And we were already out drinking on a weeknight, so I don't understand why..."

"I'm really sorry, Luce. I swear, I'm going to take the weekend. We can finally have that dinner. Please?"

"Yes. Of course."

"Are we okay?" A hint of concern had crept in.

"We are," Luce confirmed. "I'll see you then."

They had arrived at Kendra's residence, and the driver parked on the curb.

"Good. I can't wait. It's been a nice evening." They shared another quick kiss before Kendra left and walked to her front door.

It might have been the alcohol, or too much rich food, but Luce didn't feel okay at all.

How could a day go to Hell in a heartbeat? They had freed the children before they might have gone hungry, sick, or worse.

The most amazing woman she'd ever met wanted to be with her, still. What she'd been fantasizing about for some time now was likely only a few days away.

As she paced in her living room, Luce couldn't shake the antsy, tense feeling of impending doom. She had been excited about a lead in the case, not concerned about anything when the car crashed into hers, the airbag deployed, and she lost consciousness.

She hadn't spent weeks in that house of horrors, just long enough to understand the dire possibilities when ignorance was coddled too much.

There was no alcohol in the house, and she didn't feel like making another coffee with her nerves raw like this.

She'd had a dessert at the bar. There was nothing sweet in the house either. She'd have to go grocery shopping soon.

For the second time in as many days, she lay on her bed fully clothed, crying for nothing in particular, her body and mind not where it should have been.

⁂

No bagel and cottage cheese for this breakfast. Luce had spent a sleepless night, frustrated with herself for some tangible reasons, frustrated with Kendra for no good reason. Now she had to get herself back into an acceptable work mindset, because while she was indulging in her emotions, Sarah and Poppy were still out there.

Not wanting to be home either, she had settled at the counter of a coffee shop with a muffin and a specialty coffee, irrationally feeling like more than one person in her life would call her out on it if they could see her.

Her thoughts wandered back to the children, and she wondered if any of them had gotten sick on candy or dessert last night. Justin had seen Poppy on Wheeler's phone. Coincidence, or had Wheeler singled her out? Why?

The questions pressing on her mind presented a stark contrast to the sweet taste of the cheesecake filling and the whipped cream on her coffee.

Jared Hyde wouldn't get any of this in prison, though he likely wouldn't stay on the inside as long as she thought he should. He insisted to this day that he never meant to cause Wendy Tillis's death.

To many supporters of his "cause" he was still a hero and would be at the time of his release.

Luce, on the other hand, didn't think she could ever forgive anyone who had done their part for Hyde to come into the kind of power he'd had as a candidate. It wasn't just about her, the things that happened, what almost happened. There was a bigger picture, a bigger fight, and sometimes it just felt like losing was inevitable simply because too many people couldn't be bothered to acknowledge the danger. Especially when the extremist was a "friend" or someone in their family.

She was drifting, and she couldn't afford it. Luce finished her decadent breakfast, ruefully wondering what had happened to being happy and focusing on the good things in life.

Her workplace seemed reassuringly quiet. Good. The episode she'd had last night, alone in her house, had spooked her, leaving her with no doubt that everything was not okay, not yet. She had finished her mandatory sessions with the department psychiatrist a while ago. Luce knew she could be trusted to carry a gun, but there might be other issues at play.

Having to talk about them was something she hoped to avoid. She might have no choice.

"Hey." Tyler looked up from his computer screen when she sat behind her desk. "I talked to the doctor. They're cautiously optimistic that they can bring Wheeler out of the coma today. They'll call us if there's any news."

"Good. Thanks. Anything from the parents?"

"Mr. and Mrs. Dennis asked to meet with us again. They'll be in later," Ritter explained. "I thought you could take care of that? You seemed to have a good rapport."

"Of course."

She thought back to their interview with Brock yesterday. He and Layne were still their only leads on Sarah and Poppy, and both claimed they didn't know Wheeler. Who was lying? The fact that Justin might have more to say was intriguing, but they already knew that Wheeler had stalked Layne and captured him meeting Sarah.

She picked up her phone and called Matt Layne.

"Hi, this is Detective Allen. I have a few follow-up questions."

"I hear you found the children. Thank you so much, Detective. I'm so glad they're okay. They are, right? At least that's what the newspaper says."

"They'll be fine. Mr. Layne, I was wondering if there was ever a confrontation between you and Mr. Brock."

Silence. Then he sighed. "So you heard. I'm sure he told you a version very different from what really happened."

"Then what did happen, Mr. Layne?" She made no attempt at holding back her frustration. "This is important. Sarah and Poppy are still missing. I was under the impression they mattered to you."

"Of course they do!" he insisted, sounding upset. "I want them to be home. I want them to be free of that asshole. I know we were supposed to be careful, but he showed up at the school one day, and the way he was talking to her...I just couldn't stand it. Regardless of what he said, I didn't shove or punch him. I heard that was a story he told afterwards."

"And you didn't think that was important to share with us?"

"I don't know why it would matter. You've met him. Do you still doubt Sarah is in danger from him?"

Luce wasn't going to answer that question. "I assume you're going back to work soon?"

"Yes, of course. Will you let me know if you learn anything about Sarah? I'm sorry I didn't tell you about this."

"Okay. I'll get back to you later," she said when she saw Ritter making signs in her direction. "If you can think of anything else, please, call. Every detail is important."

A few minutes later, she sat once again with the Dennis family after providing the couple with coffee, and Justin with a hot chocolate.

"How are you?" she began. That was the easier part. Easier than taking a hard look at her own condition.

"We are doing okay," Leona Dennis said after sharing a look with her husband. "We've been talking about what happened, and Justin insisted that we come back here. I'm not sure..."

"Mom," he interrupted her. "I *have* to tell her."

"What is it you have to tell me?" Luce asked, her heart beating faster.

"Poppy. She was supposed to be on the bus in the morning, but she wasn't. I thought her mom and the other guy drove her to school, but then I never saw her again after that."

"That other guy?" She frowned. "Frank?"

"No, it wasn't Frank. He drove the bus that day. I saw Poppy with her mom that morning when we drove by. There was a man with them."

Luce refrained from the impulse to jump to her feet. Mr. Dennis misinterpreted her silence.

"I'm sorry if we're taking your time. Justin was upset about this."

"No, that's perfectly fine," she hurried to say. "It's all good, Justin. And you're sure it wasn't Poppy's dad? You met him once, right?"

"Yes. He came to Poppy's birthday party. He was pretty mean to her mom and after that..." He cast a look at his parents.

"Yes, your mom and dad told me about that."

"I wasn't allowed to go back," Justin said with a sigh. "Poppy and I are still friends though."

"That's good. About that man you saw with her and Ms. Burke...Can you tell me what he looked like?

"He was big. Brown hair."

"Like the man with Frank?"

"Yes, but bigger," he said. "Poppy didn't look happy."

"Justin, are you sure this is really what you saw?" Leona Dennis looked nervous. "This has been a scary time."

"Yes, but I saw them," Justin insisted. "They were in front of the house, about to get into the car."

Sarah Burke's car still sat in its parking spot. Luce had an idea.

"I know I'm asking a lot, but since you're here...Would you be up to going to Sarah and Poppy's house, and show me exactly? This could really help us."

"I don't know..." Justin's father started, while his son had no such reservations.

"It's no problem at all."

Luce cast another glance at the parents, suppressing a smile. Finally, the couple relented.

"Great. You know the address, right? I'll meet you there."

"It's not dangerous, is it? You don't think someone's watching the house?"

Unfortunately, Luce was sure that whoever had taken the two was likely far from their home.

"It's fine," she assured them. "I promise you it won't take long."

"Can we have pizza afterwards?" Justin asked, making the adults laugh, dissolving the tension.

"I have the feeling your son is a great negotiator," Luce commented. "I'll see you in a few."

Chapter Ten

B usy was good. It didn't make her feel so inadequate, like she was overlooking something, or like she was on her way to messing up the best thing that had ever happened to her. There was a risk that came with putting herself out there.

She couldn't dwell on it now.

Luce arrived first and parked her car in front of Sarah Burke's house, once again admiring the neighborhood. There was a good distance between neighbors—they had not gotten anything of use from them. But this was where Justin had seen Poppy and Sarah from the school bus.

She looked around, imagined the bus passing by, Wheeler driving. He must have been in contact with the man who abducted Sarah and Poppy. She made a mental note to call the lab later and see if they had anything new.

If only Wheeler woke up...

The Dennises arrived and parked behind Luce's car. She could tell that the parents were eager to get this over with, as if the place spooked them. Justin was also eager, but for a different reason.

"Okay, just tell me quick where they were standing."

He walked towards the front of the house, indicating the driveway. "The car was here, and they were standing next to it."

"This is very good, Justin. Can you think of anything else?"

She stared at the concrete, imploring the all-important clue to appear out of the blue. But they'd already searched the area.

Justin shook his head, for the first time looking dejected.

"Please, take your time. And you know, you and your parents can always call me if anything comes back to you. You're doing great."

Luce hoped that a bit of flattery might be encouraging. The boy was motivated, no doubt about it. He looked again at the empty spot and shook his head.

"I'm sorry, Ma'am."

"That's all right. I'll let you enjoy your pizza now. What's your favorite?" she asked, forcing a smile.

He did the same, not fooled by her attempt at distracting him.

"Pepperoni," he muttered.

"Maybe you and your parents can soon go with Sarah and Poppy," she suggested, relieved when that brought a smile to his face. Luce had lowered her voice in case his parents were not fully on board with that idea. But if it turned out that Brock was involved in the kidnappings, he'd be out of their lives for good. She hoped that once Sarah and Poppy were safely back home, both the parents and their children could move on.

"That would be great," Leona Dennis said. She had over-heard the brief exchange after all.

"Thank you," Luce addressed the family. "Have a good day."

She waited until they had left, then walked around the area some more. The crew had been over every square inch. The perpetrators had been careful, but within limits. They had found Frank Reilly's true identity, though it seemed they were always one step behind.

If Wheeler woke up, would he talk?

Luce walked through the gate and the backyard, unsure what she was hoping to find here. They had come through the front.

The cameras should have caught them, unless someone had messed with them.

The possibilities were giving her a headache. At times it seemed like a sophisticated operation, at other times it looked like someone had dropped the ball. What was the end game?

She jumped when her cell phone rang, realizing how silent it was back here. She couldn't help thinking of Justin's parents' concerns that the perpetrators might return to the scene of the crime.

Luce still didn't think it was an issue, but her palms were sweating when she picked up the phone.

Driving across town in the pouring rain, talking to Tyler on the phone about the new evidence, the next steps...thinking of a silly argument she'd had with Kendra. The crossroads. Red lights...And the crash.

"Allen," she said. "What is it?"

"You are not in a good mood today, are you?" Carrie Brayden asked. "Let's see if I can make it better. We've been going over Wheeler's phone records."

"Did he call Brock?"

"No, he didn't." Carrie sighed. "That would be too easy, you know?"

"Do you have something for me or not?"

"Why would I call you otherwise? There's a number he called multiple times, a few times at the beginning of the month, then more often in the week before, and on the day of the abduction. During the same time period, several calls were made from that number to Brock headquarters."

"The middle man!" Luce exclaimed. "Carrie, you're the best."

"I know."

"Do we know who it belongs to?"

"That's a bit tricky. It's registered to a John Smith."

Luce snorted as she started to walk back to her car.

"Right. But we know for sure John Smith was in constant contact with Wheeler and Brock. I'm sure you can do something with that."

"Thank you so much. Excuse me, I have another call coming in. Talk to you later." She allowed herself a moment of excitement over the news before she addressed the next caller. "Hey, Tyler."

"Wheeler is awake," he said without preamble. "Do you have anything new?"

"Not much from Justin, but I was just on the phone with Carrie. It's good. I'll tell you when I'm there."

She unlocked her car and sat in the driver's seat, taking a deep breath. The strands were about to unravel. They'd solve this case, maybe within the next twenty-four hours.

And she would apologize to Kendra.

⁂

Wheeler was still weak, but alert enough to glare at them when they walked into the room.

"I have nothing to say to you." He coughed.

"Let's not start on the wrong foot," Tyler suggested in the jovial tone he reserved for a particular kind of suspects. "Look, man, I'm not going to give you a load of bullshit about how you can help us, and we can help you. We already have enough on you, so you'll go straight to jail as soon as the doctors give their okay."

"Then why are you here?" Wheeler scoffed.

"Good question, right, Detective Allen?" Tyler turned to her, and Luce suppressed a smile. "Smart question," he added. "Let's take it back a step. You replaced the regular driver, handed out spiked brownies to a dozen kids and locked them into a room on a construction site. They identified you. We have your prints in 'Frank Reilly's apartment. That's done. You want my honest opinion?"

Wheeler's stare said that he didn't, but didn't have much of a choice either.

"I wouldn't mind if you go down for all of it, and I don't think my colleague would either. But it's in our interest to get your accomplices off the street as well, and you...you don't want to be the last to cooperate. Especially when your buddies have the more expensive lawyers."

A bit of fishing was part of the plan, Luce knew. They had strategized for this interrogation on the way.

"Think about it. When kids are involved, that's always a tough thing to explain to the folks on your cell block. No one likes that."

Luce wasn't sure whether it was real alarm or indignation in Wheeler's expression, but the words had found their mark.

"Stop that crap. I didn't touch those kids. They had food and a bathroom."

"A few chairs and blankets, not enough for all of them, food for maybe two, three days. The toilet wasn't working. Would anyone have revealed their location?"

He shrugged. "As soon as they started the work again on the site, they would have found them eventually."

Eventually. She pushed back her anger, and the image of the frightened eyes on her. The children.

Rachel. Dawn. Cory...

"You drugged them. One of the kids had a bruise."

"That wasn't me! She bit him."

"Who?" Tyler's tone was a bit less conversational now.

"I don't know his name, they only called him Jack. That's all I know. That was the whole point. He said everything would be taken care of with the school, the other driver would be out

81

of commission, and they gave me the ID of a guy who was on vacation. I matched the photo well enough, and all I had to do was to show up and drive."

"Was he in on it, the guy whose ID you had? Anyone else from the bus company?"

"I don't think so. They hacked into their computers, set it all up so that calls to his number would go to my phone. I did what they asked, Jack and I got the kids to the site, the girl bit him and he hit her. We locked them in and left."

"Was it Jack who shot you?"

He shook his head. "No. Some other guy."

"The one who abducted Sarah and Poppy Burke? We know about that too."

"He never introduced himself, though I saw him around. Fucker came in and just shot me! I assume you're going to protect me?"

"Of course, Mr. Wheeler. That will work even better if you give us a description of him. The more detailed, the better."

With that sketch, they'd go back to Justin.

"Okay. Before we get started on that, there's one more thing."

❦

D.A. Troy listened to everything she presented without any comment, only giving a small nod here and there. So far so good, Luce hoped. Based on experience, she had expected the woman to interrupt her more often. In the aftermath of that one confrontation, they had remained polite with each other.

After her abduction, to Luce's chagrin, she'd been on the other end of the D.A.'s sympathy.

"This sounds solid to me," Troy said when Luce had finished. "Don't look so surprised. Those records tell a story, and if I'm not mistaken, a mother and her child are still missing."

"That's correct."

It wasn't always sympathy though. Luce had also received backhanded compliments and thinly veiled criticism before, but that didn't come unexpected. Ironically, she was more comfortable with the latter. She knew how to deal with that.

"Okay, let's bring him in," Chomsky declared. "And get some answers."

An hour later, both Brock and his lawyer were livid with what Luce thought was mostly manufactured outrage.

"This is rising to the level of harassment. My client has helped you every way he possibly could, and he's in sincere distress over his daughter's missing. It's still unclear what actions his wife has taken, but you don't seem to care about that."

"We can assure you we are following every lead," Luce said, resisting the urge to form fists under the table. As usual, neither man showed real concern for the victims. Sometimes she envied Tyler's calm ways, but then again, he was rarely the target of their disdain. As a cop, on occasion, as a straight white man, they considered him one of them, like Wheeler who had been rather easily fooled.

Brock, however, wouldn't go down that easily.

"And there's one of them that has been concerning to us," she continued. "We could trace Adam Wheeler's contacts, including one who made a lot of phone calls...to you. We hope you can explain this to us."

"Are you serious? A lot of people speak to Mr. Brock."

"A lot of people don't plan and execute the abduction of twelve 3rd graders," Tyler returned.

"All right." With an exaggerated sigh, Brock raised his hands. "I should have told you. I didn't want to make things worse for Sarah and Poppy. I took this...individual's call because they asked for a ransom. Wouldn't surprise me if Layne was behind this, and he and Sarah had planned this all along to make me look bad."

Luce couldn't help shaking her head. He seemed proud. It all sounded pathetic to her, but at least she had another ace up her sleeve.

"The thing is we already know that's not true. There was no ransom, because that was never the plan. A bus full of children, that's guaranteed to keep the police, the press, and the public occupied. It wasn't such a bad plan, but then there were glitches in the execution."

"I have no idea what the hell you're talking about. I've indulged this long enough, and you know what, Detective Allen? I know you. Yes, I did my research as well, and I know you have an agenda. It's certainly not about the children's well-being."

Luce knew what was coming, and it was the only thing that kept her from responding.

When Brock jumped to his feet, Tyler laid a hand on his shoulder, picking up his cuffs with the other one.

"Mr. Brock, you are under arrest for suspicion of the abduction of Sarah and Poppy Burke, and twelve other children." He calmly continued the familiar words over the other men's outrage.

"You fucking bet I can afford an attorney, and you are both going to lose your jobs! Fucking incompetent leftists!"

At this point, his lawyer tried to calm him down, to little avail.

"I will need some time to confer with my client," he said.

"I'm sure you will," Luce agreed. "Once we're done. You know how this works. An officer will take Mr. Brock to booking, and I assume the bail hearing could be as early as tomorrow morning."

Brock opened his mouth but refrained from commenting. His attorney spoke for him instead.

"I am confident that my client will be out of here within the hour."

Unfortunately, Luce thought, it wasn't that unlikely. They just had to work faster.

When they were alone in the room, Tyler slumped into a chair, bursting out laughing.

"'Fucking leftists'? What kind of schoolyard insult was that? Wow."

"You're still surprised that people like him aren't the most mature?" she asked mildly.

"Not really. Let's get this show on the road before he makes good on his threats. That lawyer's car is worth more than what you and I earn in a year. Together."

"Talk about priorities." She laughed.

A knock on the door preceded D.A. Troy into the room, her arrival putting both of them in a more sober mood.

"I trust that you have your ducks in a row," she said.

Luce refrained from the childish impulse to roll her eyes.

"He lied about the ransom. We have those records. Wheeler's statement."

"You can't put him at the scene yet."

"He wasn't there. Justin Dennis, one of the children from the bus, saw a man with Sarah and Poppy. Wheeler described him to us, and I'm certain Justin will confirm. Once we have him..."

"Yeah, get started on that. And get a bit more out of Brock while you're at it. He's well regarded in the conservative business community, and a big donor."

Luce suppressed a wry smile at Tyler's warning glance. He had seen her on a confrontational course with the D.A., but she knew what was on the line.

"We'll get it done," she simply said. Maybe she was simply too tired to argue about the many ways men like Brock were coddled, given a head start from birth. It had not done her that much good. And the D.A. had a point, unfortunately, by pointing out that their job wasn't done.

"I'll call Mr. and Mrs. Dennis," she said.

Chapter Eleven

Justin was quick to confirm that the sketch they had, thanks to Adam Wheeler, looked exactly like the man he had seen outside Sarah Burke's house. Good. Luce hoped they'd be able to get the whole story from Brock before he went before the judge, and then his attorney and the D.A. could hash out whatever they thought was possible.

At this point, she couldn't even bring herself to rage against a machine that would likely come up with something favorable for him. Conservative donors. D.A. Troy walked that world too, and she might be just as disgusted over what he had done, but aiming at a run for office herself, she wouldn't rock the boat too hard.

"What's with the glum look?" Ritter asked when she had ended the call. "Things are moving. Aren't you happy about that?"

Happy, she had been last night, at least for a while. Since that near-breakdown, something was starting to catch up with her. The case. Life in general. Not so distant memories, perhaps.

"I am. We still don't know where they are."

He shrugged. "Even he will figure out the gravity of his situation at some point."

"From your mouth to God's ears...or whoever will listen."

She cast a look at her watch. Luce wished she could take a quick moment to call Kendra, but unfortunately that too would have to wait.

Luce went home late, frustrated. They didn't have any leads on Sarah and Poppy, Brock was clamming up, and it was too late to bother Kendra with her worries. She didn't feel like going home either but instead stopped at a diner where she ordered a coffee and a piece of banana cream pie that would serve as dinner.

Happy. Why wasn't she? She had so much to look forward to, thanks to…Women who had been strangers until the moment they were thrown together into a possibly fatal situation, colleagues who had tirelessly worked to find her, and Kendra whose warmth and affection had gone a long way to ease the nightmares afterwards.

Why wasn't it enough?

Luce knew that Sarah and Poppy's fate didn't lie only in her hands, that she was doing everything she could. She didn't suffer from survivor's guilt, because she knew she had done her part, fought to survive, to get that second chance.

Even as she listed her accomplishments and blessings, the world in front of her looked bleak. Save for that coffee and pie. The rich, sweet taste was a welcome distraction.

She couldn't go on like this.

Luce hadn't missed the fact that not drinking didn't mean she was on her way to developing a less than healthy habit.

She wasn't sure how to stop it, or when, but certainly not tonight.

Luce spent most of the night awake, pondering how she could find some distance. It was no secret why Brock had her on edge, but that didn't help anyone, least of all Sarah and Poppy.

He had been in contact with a man who had hired Wheeler to execute the abduction of the children on the bus, according to Wheeler, a distraction gone wrong. He had overheard some shouting between the man whose identity he didn't know, and Brock.

The original plan was to have everyone assume that Poppy had been on the school bus to stall the authorities—but the timeline had been off.

John Smith had returned to Wheeler's apartment to tie up loose ends.

There was another missing accomplice, the infamous Jack who had hit Caitlyn for biting him. Luce assumed that like Wheeler, he was one of the hired goons. The connection between Brock and John Smith was more interesting. How had the construction mogul found him? Did he already have ties to organized crime?

They might have to call in more reinforcements on this one. Luce gazed outside the window. It was still pitch dark, the quiet of the night heavy. With a sigh, she got up to make herself more coffee.

Brock's finances might tell the story, but given his extensive wealth and property, that might take a while. What if Sarah and Poppy ran out of supplies meanwhile, like the children almost had?

❦

As she was getting ready for work, the fact that it was Saturday almost slipped her mind. Luce would go in for a couple of hours to check on the progress. After that, she couldn't stall any longer, especially when this was supposed to be the weekend...

Any romantic activities were far from her mind after the almost all-nighter. After the amount of coffee she'd had between the diner, and the hours afterwards, breakfast didn't appeal to her either. Maybe later.

Luce made her rounds at the station, checked in with Lieutenant Chomsky and the lab. Both Ritter's and Murphy's desks were empty. Everyone had her number and would call her if something of importance happened.

She went over every detail of her notes and report before she sat back in her car, taking a deep breath before she called the number.

"Hi, Luce," Kendra's voice came over the line a moment later. "How are you?"

The audible concern nearly broke something within her, the idea frightening. She had kept it together so well. Mostly. Time had passed, she had to be ready to move on with life, wasn't she? Especially when it had so much to offer.

Time to take responsibility.

"I wanted to say I'm really sorry. I don't know what happened the other night." Kendra was silent for a few seconds, and Luce had the uncomfortable impression that she knew exactly what happened. "Will you forgive me?" She wasn't even joking.

"There's nothing to forgive, Luce. You know, I've been thinking a lot about the day we met. It was all chaos, and really scary..."

That surprised her. When Luce came to the clinic where the evacuation due to a bomb threat was under way, Kendra had been the most calm and efficient person on the scene, making her own job so much easier.

"You didn't seem scared."

"Oh, I was, no matter how many threats we get. It's not something you get used to. Scared, angry, all of the above. I'll never forget how you made me feel safe that day. I was so happy we became friends...but I've had a crush on you for a long time." She laughed a little as if self-conscious. Luce knew better. Kendra didn't say things she didn't mean. She wasn't that type of person.

"No, that's bad. It's so much more than a crush."

"I'm...flattered, but what does that have to do with my screw-up?"

"You don't have to worry about anything." She sounded serious now. "I am not backing out, I promise you. Maybe I was the one who needed a bit more time, because I've wanted this for so long."

"You don't have to worry either. I'm not going anywhere."

Luce wanted to say something else, but it was much too early for that, and she wasn't good at saying it under the best of circumstances. She had to find the perfect moment for it, and it sure wasn't now. However...

"I skipped breakfast this morning...Yes, I know," she added quickly before Kendra could gently call her out on this questionable habit, like she did on occasion. "I was wondering if you'd like to come over for an early lunch, or, I don't know, brunch? Whatever."

How irresponsible of you, that little voice nagged. Having brunch while those women are forced to have soup and stale bread. This time, her meddling subconscious was too obvious for her to fall for it.

She needed food. She needed Kendra's calm, warm presence.

When Kendra said "I'd love to. Can I bring anything?" the relief was staggering.

⟊

Letting Kendra choose the food wasn't a matter of laziness, but an honest attempt to do better on Luce's part. Meanwhile, she set the table, even adding blue napkins she couldn't remember buying.

Something had to give at some point. But she still had to live her life, that new promising life she had been granted.

When she opened the door, Kendra went straight into her hug, and they just stood for a few seconds. She reveled in the warmth until Kendra pulled back and put the bags she'd brought on the side table.

"Good morning, Detective."

"It is now, Doctor."

They laughed at the kind of silliness they allowed themselves rarely.

"Come on in. I'm hungry."

"Yeah? It's a good thing I have everything you need."

How could she continue to be glum, as Ritter had put it yesterday, when this extraordinary woman was with her, her tone all flirty and full of suggestion?

"I don't doubt it."

"Good."

Kendra reached out to cup her face in both hands, the tender gesture eliciting a gasp. She might still be dreaming. There was rarely time in her life for any of this. As long as Luce had known Kendra, she would always make time for a friend in need, or her patients, but that seemed to pretty much fill up her time.

But they weren't just friends any longer, and need...it had a different meaning at this moment.

"I missed you," Kendra whispered, and to make sure she knew the feeling was mutual, Luce kissed her. Softly at first, more deeply when Kendra showed her appreciation. Her hands, stealing under Luce's shirt, caused a blissful shiver, and everything that weighed heavily on her fell away.

Brunch could wait. This couldn't. The new red couch she had bought after renovations were finished in this room was closest. Her shirt came off altogether, and Luce was happy to return the favor. They kissed again, and this time her mouth went to Kendra's neck, her hands eagerly exploring her body like she had wanted for longer than she had been able to admit to herself.

Kendra didn't doubt her, or what they could be together. She had said so. Luce would tell her when the moment was right, but she had always felt safe with her too, after a tough day, after an experience that kept haunting her, and right now.

She found herself on her back, her body thrumming with heat and anticipation.

"There's something I should tell you," she mumbled, admiring Kendra swiftly undoing her belt. Her heart was racing.

"It's all right. I don't have any hang-ups about being someone's first."

Luce couldn't help laughing. "I'm sorry, that's not what I meant. I've dated women before." Kendra's calm gaze on her made the next part possible too. "I just wasn't in love with them...until now."

For a split-second, panic filled her mind. Had she really said that out loud? This wasn't like her. Would Kendra think of it as juvenile? Luce had no time to cringe as Kendra's lips were on hers the next moments, her hand slipping past the waistband of Luce's jeans, bringing her to a mindset that was very much adult and leaving no room for anything but glorious pleasure.

"Works for me," she whispered.

It was working for Luce, too. Perfectly.

Chapter Twelve

When she pulled the comforter over them later, and Kendra snuggled into her arms, Luce had no idea what had held her back, in the recent past, or before that. How could she have thought it might be complicated?

In fact, this seemed the only part of her life that was blessedly uncomplicated, not laden by pressing decisions or past mistakes. She wished they could have stayed here forever.

"I swear this was not what I had planned, at least not as soon as I got here." Kendra laughed softly. "I don't regret it though."

"Me neither," Luce admitted, before she leaned in to kiss her. Her growling stomach reminded her that she still hadn't had breakfast.

"I'm glad. But I was going to make sure you had a decent meal, and that's still on the agenda. Um...you will have to move first."

Being chivalrous enough to leave Kendra the blanket, Luce got up to collect her clothes, aware of her admiring gaze. She couldn't help smiling.

"You like what you see?"

"You have no idea."

Luce realized she wouldn't have the last word on this, and she didn't mind. When she was halfway decent, she collected Kendra's clothes as well and handed them to her.

"I'm going to make some coffee then. I can't wait to see what you brought."

"It's not cottage cheese today, I promise."

"Oh. It will be indulgent?"

Kendra got to her feet, still clad in the comforter.

"I promise. We work our behinds off to make a tiny difference. We deserve indulgence, even when the other side never stops."

It sounded reasonable to Luce.

Yet, as she was preparing the coffee, she couldn't help thinking of Sarah. Had she found a good relationship with Matt Layne? Was he serious when he said he was worried about her, wanted to protect her? Luce hoped that was the case, and they could find some normalcy after Sarah and Poppy returned.

It wasn't just her. Everyone deserved that.

Kendra, now dressed again, brought her bags into the kitchen. They contained buttery croissants, jam, orange juice, some cheese and grapes. At this point, the sight nearly made her knees buckle.

Luce didn't want to go there again, but she remembered how Kendra had often cooked for her after the rescue. Maybe at some point, no matter how well intentioned and kind, it had made her feel like she wasn't doing enough, like she wasn't carrying her weight in their relationship.

But she was never going back there.

"Thank you. This is amazing."

"You believe me now, don't you?"

She couldn't seem to keep the smile off her face. This was so different from the way she had usually approached relationships, moving in and out of people's lives with no intention of staying because she couldn't imagine why they would care enough to want to keep her there. Pathetic, really. She had only herself to blame.

With Kendra, everything had been different from the start.

"I do," she said. "I swear. You know I'm really good at figuring out if someone's telling the truth."

Everything was as perfect as it possibly could be. After a rather decadent brunch, they took a walk in the park near Luce's house, something they, for some reason, had never taken the time for before.

Or perhaps this was a special moment, the beginning of something amazing...Reality caught up with them in the afternoon when Kendra' cell phone rang.

"I have to get this," she said, her expression apologetic. Luce nodded, understanding calls out of the blue. Her hopes that this could be solved quickly were squashed when she saw the horror on Kendra's face.

"Oh my God. I'll be there as soon as I can. Damn." She had already ended the call when she said the last word. Getting up and gathering her purse and coat, Kendra continued, "I hate to leave like this, but I'll call you later, okay? It's one of my patients. I need to see her right away."

"It's okay. I'll be here. Should I drive you?" Luce suggested. She sensed something different about Kendra. She had rarely seen her this upset. Even when she had come to see Luce in the hospital that other time, she never projected anything but calm and supportive. She had seen her at work. This was...alarming.

"No. No, I'll be fine. I just have to go. I'll take to you later." She placed a quick kiss on Luce's lips and was gone before Luce could even think of seeing her to the door.

There was nothing she could do but wait, so she decided to take care of the dishes. Maybe call Jill.

Maybe take a quick tour to the station and see where everyone was at.

⟨⟨⟨⟩⟩⟩

The last thing Luce had expected was to get a call from Brock's lawyer on her cell phone. The day was getting more and more confusing, the beautiful parts fading further into the distance, like a dream.

"Where did you get this number?" she asked, both irritated and excited. That could only mean one thing: Movement.

"I don't recall. It's really not important. If you want to help reunite Mr. Brock with his daughter, you should come here right now. I'm with him. He wants to talk to you."

Was he serious? Would they finally learn what happened to Sarah and Poppy?

"I hope you're not going to waste anyone's time," she warned.

"That's not Mr. Brock's intention, or mine."

"Good. I'm calling D.A. Troy first."

"Do what you must, then get over here. Time is of the essence."

"No. You'll have to come to the station." She wasn't going to risk Brock walking away on a technicality. This had to be by the book.

"Fine," he snapped and hung up before Luce could ask any more questions.

She was in the car a few minutes later, calling D.A. Troy using Bluetooth.

"On a Saturday," she remarked, a trace of sarcasm to her voice. "To what do I owe the honor, Detective?"

"Brock wants to talk." Luce ignored the subtle hint that the two didn't exactly socialize...on Saturdays, or ever, if they could avoid it. "I'm sure your presence could be an additional incentive."

"Really? I don't think we can offer him anything else with what we already know. Those children might be traumatized for life."

"I understand that, but Sarah Burke and Poppy are still out there."

"Yes." Troy sighed. "I know. I'll be there."

"Thank you. I hope we can do this quickly."

"You and me both. I have somewhere to be later tonight."

Luce didn't ask. She liked the relative peace between them. It was convenient—and less stressful than the alternative. Lieutenant Chomsky would be so proud of her.

Luce was a long way from being proud of herself when she sat across Brock and his lawyer in the interrogation room, with Troy and Chomsky watching from the other side. She had called Tyler as well but only reached his voicemail.

The pressure was mounting.

"Mr. Brock, this had better be good. Your attorney tells me you have something to say. Do you know where Sarah and Poppy are?"

"No, I don't."

She realized that he looked aged. Did the man actually feel remorse? Why was he still lying then?

"Come on, I don't have time for this."

"It's true!" he insisted. "I made sure they were both in a safe place, where Sarah would have time to think and come to the right conclusions."

The tone was more familiar, though she didn't know what to make of his words other than they creeped her out. The right conclusions.

"What does that mean? You locked her in somewhere, so she'd hand custody of Poppy over to you?"

"You don't get it," he said with a lot more disdain than a man in his situation should be able to muster.

"Then enlighten me."

"I thought that if she and Poppy had a quiet space, she would be able to let go of the past. I could forgive her mistakes, and she'd come back to me."

All of a sudden, she found it hard to breathe. Was he about to confess a murder? Damn it, no. Not today. She couldn't deal with it. She didn't want to. Luce was almost sure that if it came down to that, she would hand in her resignation, walk out of here and never look back.

She'd had it, was done with men who didn't take no for an answer, wanted to dictate every aspect of a woman's life—because in their mind, all women belonged to them. Even the attorney summoning her here was a display of that attitude.

"Sarah didn't want to come back to you though. She has her own life, with Poppy—and with Matt Layne."

"Did he tell you that? That pathetic little—"

"Mr. Brock, why are we here?"

"I paid someone to look after Sarah and Poppy," he had raised his tone as well, his face reddening, and the attorney placed a hand on his shoulder. "They made a live feed available to me."

"Where are they?"

She was still torn between rage and excitement. They could bring them home today.

"I don't know. That was the whole point. Once Sarah was ready to see reason, he would let them go."

"And marriage counseling never occurred to you?" Sarcasm was a thin lifeline at this moment. She had been right about him from the start. He had used his money to execute a Machiavellian plan, but it was even worse than she imagined, even more nefarious. "Why would you make an arrangement like that in the first place?"

"It was supposed to be safe! But now I can't reach him, and the feed is dead. I'm sure he knows that you arrested me." Anger was blazing in his eyes once more. "If anything happens to them, it's on you. I'm going to sue the entire department..."

"Mr. Brock."

"This is not going to end well for you if they get hurt."

"You are hardly in the position to sue anyone," Luce said coldly. "I need every single detail about this arrangement, how you approached him, every single thing he told you. I assume you can show me the feed. Did you record anything?"

The attorney looked uncomfortable.

"Of course. I have the feed from each day. That was part of the deal."

"What about the school bus?"

He made a dismissive gesture.

"Idiot screwed that up and took my money. Those kids should have been all right for at least a week. They were supposed to make it look like Poppy was on the bus, and for sure they were not supposed to leave any clues in that damn apartment."

If it wasn't for those prints, they might not have gotten to Wheeler, which meant a dozen 3rd graders in a cold room, dwindling supplies and a non-functioning bathroom.

"All right. I need that information *now*."

Chapter Thirteen

L uce and Tyler went to an empty conference room to start watching the recorded feed from where Sarah and Poppy Burke were held. Luce's stomach did a flip-flop when she saw the white walls and non-descript furniture. Not because she knew the place, but because the looks of it were oddly reminiscent.

The woman and child in the video sat at a table, talking in quiet hushed tones. To an uninformed observer, this might look like a normal scene, but knowing the circumstances, the weight of fear and responsibility was undeniable.

"We'll be okay," Sarah said to Poppy. *"Daddy is coming to get us in a few days like he promised."*

Except Daddy had no idea where they were held. It made sense, to some extent—from his point of view, since it gave him plausible deniability.

Luce could read between the lines. The man for the job, "John Smith" had been involved in some extortion schemes and intimidation of competitors. When Brock realized Sarah wasn't coming back to him just because he asked, he hired "Smith" to play a part in the convincing.

As pathetic as all of this was, they had a job to do now. Troy confirmed that depending on the findings, they might add charges for Brock, and everyone involved in said schemes, but Sarah and Poppy were their priority.

"I believe in traditional marriage," he had the brazenness to say, a thrice-married, twice-divorced man who couldn't keep a wife unless he held her hostage.

Luce focused her attention on the screen. The man came in sporadically to bring food and water, but he made sure that the camera only captured him from the back. He also wore a mask, all black clothes, and boots.

She noticed that Poppy seemed to forget about the dire situation every once in a while, when Sarah tried to engage her in a game, but she was clearly afraid of the man. With reason. Every time he came into the room, he was carrying a rifle. He never spoke, just dropped the supplies and left again.

There was no hesitation, no sign of nervousness. John Smith wasn't an amateur. He must have done similar jobs before.

"Are you okay?" Tyler asked into the relative silence.

"Not really," she admitted. So far, the scenes on the screen kept repeating themselves. Sometimes, when Poppy was sleeping, Sarah addressed the camera.

"I don't know what you're trying to achieve with this, but we're over. Can't we keep it civil for Poppy? I know you care about her."

Enough to have a stranger kidnap her and her mother, putting their lives into the hands of a man who was wanted for attempted murder. One attempted murder that they knew of.

"I will be once we find them," she added. "I can't believe that we've learned so much more only to hit a wall again. This was all done on purpose. There's nothing identifiable in that video."

"Clearly."

Tyler's own frustration came through in the single word. "I think we'll be at this for a while. Care for a coffee?"

"Sure."

He shook his head when she reached for her wallet.

"I got it."

"Okay. Thanks."

When the door opened only a few minutes later, she thought he might have forgotten his, but instead an officer walked in with an unfamiliar woman. Her blonde hair came down to her shoulders in stylish waves, and Luce couldn't help admiring her coat.

"Oh. I was told Tyler was here," she said with a pleasant smile. "I see I missed him. You must be Luce, right? I'm..."

"Susan." The last thing Luce expected today was to meet his ex-wife. She got to her feet and stood, feeling every bit as awkward as she would have predicted. The officer gave her a questioning look. She nodded to him, so he left. "Luce Allen. Nice to meet you. Tyler went to get some coffee, but it's not far. He should be back any minute."

Luce should not be rambling. She and Tyler had both moved on, he with his ex, Luce with the person who had been her best friend in the past year, but had always meant so much more to her.

Still, they had a bit of a history between them which was all fine as long as things stayed professional, and they didn't bring it up. Before she could figure out what to say next, Tyler returned from his coffee run, smiling at the visitor.

"Hey. I didn't know you were coming. I would have brought you one." They kissed, and Luce turned her attention back to her screen.

"You can have mine if you have something to talk about..." she offered.

He laughed. "Nah, you get grumpy when you're undercaffeinated, and Susan likes her coffee black."

"All right then," she mumbled. "Thanks. I'll just...get back to this."

"I didn't mean to disturb you," Susan said. "If you just have a minute?"

"Of course. I'll be right back," he addressed Luce.

The two of them left, and Luce breathed a sigh of relief. She went back to the feed, thinking that before, she always used to have her coffee black. Some experiences changed a person. In various ways.

Having access to Brock's finances was a double-edged sword, Luce thought when she trudged to her car wearily. It was late...again. After the initial excitement that came with this confession, a sense of sobriety had set in. They'd need more personnel on this, having a mind-boggling amount of data to go through.

The amount of revenue he had made in the past few years was staggering. Sarah seemed to live comfortably with her daughter in a wealthy neighborhood, but it was no comparison to her ex-husband's riches. He might be involved in illegal activities beyond the ones he had admitted. Luce tended to believe that he might not even know about all of them, having delegated them a long time ago.

He would know about threats to competitors, intimidation, but not necessarily details. He was smart, protecting himself so he wouldn't take the fall. Someone had outsmarted him.

"John Smith."

As she drove home, she wondered how Kendra's day had gone. There was no message which was unusual. Given the environment they both worked in, and recent events, checking in had become a habit for them.

After parking her car in front of her house, Luce picked up her phone to write a text, then decided against it, put her seat belt back on and pulled out of the spot.

Call it intuition, but she felt that the conversation would be better done in person. It might be nothing. In that case, Luce would be excited to share the progress they'd made in the case.

She wasn't kidding herself. She just wanted to see Kendra.

The thought put a smile on her face, and she allowed herself a moment of gratitude, for interactions that hadn't been as awkward as they could have been, for that someone in her life who cared about her more than anyone, something she had thought to be impossible.

Luce cared about her too, and she was no longer afraid to acknowledge how much.

Because there were so many other things to be more afraid of, but that was beside the point.

The lights were on at Kendra's. She rang the doorbell, her heart beating faster with every passing second—for various reasons.

The moment Kendra opened the door, Luce knew for sure the evening wouldn't proceed in the same fashion as the glorious morning they'd shared. Her face was tear-streaked, her eyes welling up again when Luce walked inside, softly closing the door behind her before she pulled her close.

"What's wrong?"

"I lost her," Kendra whispered, the few words encompassing a world of raw and conflicting emotions.

"I'm so sorry." Luce held her tight, aware of all the implications, for the two of them in this moment, and beyond. Kendra had held her up when she wasn't sure how to move on from recent experiences, too angry at a world that produced men like Jared Hyde. She had to take a step back from her own story. She had to step up. "Let's sit, okay? Do you want to talk about it?"

Kendra took a deep breath.

"I think I want to wash my face first. I'm sorry. I really didn't want you to see me like this...but I'm glad you're here."

"I'll focus on the latter part," Luce said, encouraged when she got a small smile in return. "And I won't even start about the state you've seen me in. I can't begin to imagine how hard this is for you."

Luce had dealt with traumatized victims of crime, her own guilt. She followed Kendra into the living room where the latter took a tissue from an already half-depleted box. She had a glass of wine on the table. Not a bottle, Luce noticed.

They both had their areas to be careful about. Chocolate cake. Red wine. They tried, and mostly succeeded, not to slide into something unhealthy, though Luce felt like it had been more challenging recently, at least for her.

"The worst about this is, it's not even that surprising, and I hate that I even think about it this way. We could have helped her, had she come to us earlier. But she didn't know, was afraid and ashamed, and it was too late."

Luce waited, listening. She could remember many conversations between them, wondering how Kendra managed to keep doing what she did, in the face of obtuse and dangerous opposition from politicians, the uninformed, and the willfully ignorant, some of which paraded up and down outside her workplace with guns.

Yes, she had a point telling Luce that anger would mostly serve to bring up a person's blood pressure, not create a solution. Luce could testify about the blood pressure results, but for her, anger had served as an anchor, something that kept her going when she couldn't always succeed. It seemed that Kendra wasn't completely immune.

"It's not your fault," she said. Kendra certainly knew that, but words mattered. Saying them out loud mattered.

"Yes, I know. She was too far gone by the time they brought her in. Sepsis. Her mother prayed for me, her father yelled at me for an hour straight." She shook her head. "It probably wasn't that long, but it felt like it."

"I hear you." She did. In the long run, all they could do was keep their heads down, do their jobs and whatever civic duty they were able to perform as the same politicians kept aiming for voting rights as well.

Kendra's smile was a bit more genuine. "I know you do. And I appreciate very much that you haven't said, 'I told you so.'"

"I might have yelled back at him, but I know that's not you."

"I was tempted," Kendra admitted. "What fucked up kind of parent raises their kid in a setting of fear and submission? That's not faith. I know people of faith. I have my own. Imagine creating a completely hopeless situation for your child, in which they can never trust you, and when the worst happens, you blame the stranger who actually tried to save her. I can deal with the folks outside any day of the week. I walk inside and do my job. This has been more intrusive than anything I've seen in a while. I let it get to me."

"I don't blame you for that either. And I want you to know I'm here for you. Whatever you need to do, I don't know, a ritual..." Despite her good intentions, Luce felt slightly out of her depth.

"That's okay. I just need a bit of time," Kendra reasoned. "I know that the best way to honor her is to keep doing the work and hoping, against all reason, that it will get better."

Luce figured it wasn't the right moment to bring up the makeup of the Supreme Court, voting, or another reason why they likely needed to be extremely patient—and cautious in the years to come. Regardless...

"We've survived so far, haven't we?" It wasn't something she offered lightly. Between bomb threats and a car crash and subsequent abduction, they had beaten the odds in a significant way. And it was mostly thanks to Kendra that she had been able to shift her thoughts to this place from the initial feeling of utter helplessness. "Speaking of which, have you eaten anything?"

"Hm, that's my line, usually."

"Don't try to divert from the subject," Luce chided gently. "Have you?"

"I can't lie to you, which gives me a lot of confidence in the way you're doing your job, Detective Allen."

"That's flattering, but I happen to know you're a bad liar. You're also the most beautiful and compassionate person I know, and you don't deserve this. I can't undo any of it, much as I wish, but I can make you dinner."

The way Kendra's eyes widened might be an indication she had less confidence in Luce's cooking than her interrogation skills.

"Don't worry. I'm not overestimating myself. I've been known to cook my own meals on occasion." To be fair, it hadn't happened all that often since she had joined Special Crimes, but the basics certainly remained the same. "How about I check your fridge and pantry, and I'll make us something?"

Kendra was clearly exhausted, but Luce could tell she was intrigued.

"We could just order something."

"Let me give it a try, okay? Can I get you anything else?"

"No, but thank you. I'll just have another one," she lifted her glass, "With dinner. I'm curious."

"Yeah, you and me both."

In the kitchen, Luce was relieved she hadn't promised too much when she found a can of tomato soup and a block of cheese in the fridge. A few slices of bread, butter, some cream and cilantro to dress up the soup, and they'd be all set.

Kendra joined her in the kitchen to set the table and pour another glass for herself. She took out another glass.

"If you want..."

"No, thank you." One thing at a time, Luce decided. "It won't be long."

She caught Kendra's gaze on her, soft and affectionate. She couldn't deny it—she had made a few good decisions lately.

Chapter Fourteen

I n the past year, Luce had spent many evenings with Kendra, sometimes after a tough day at work, hers, or Kendra's. Sometimes, she had slept in Kendra's bed afterwards. They enjoyed each other's company.

Between friends, it should be like that, easy. But there had always been something else between the lines, questions, dreams. It didn't matter all that much tonight, because they had already admitted the truth. No more distance. Sleeping in each other's arms had become natural even before they took it that one step further. It was what they both needed. To hold. To be held.

It would get better. In many ways, it already had.

"I wish you'd move in with me," Kendra whispered, but then she didn't follow up on it. Luce wasn't sure if she had made it up, so she didn't comment either, though it was a nice thought.

❧

Back to the grind, and the recordings. They were almost done, and regardless of how hopeful Luce felt about her private life these days, she was losing hope when it came to finding Sarah and Poppy in time.

Their abductor had already made it clear that he didn't shy away from murder to tie up loose ends. He didn't seem interested in coming back and finishing the job, but that might mean he was already far away. Would he care about a woman and a child, especially now that he had cut ties to his "employer"? It wasn't likely.

They were still going through tons of documents, trying to find the connection between Brock and John Smith. How had he known to offer his services to Brock? He must have been aware that Brock was willing to commit crimes to get his way.

What if it wasn't related to the construction business at all?

Impossible, Luce decided. The fact that the children had been hidden on the site was significant. Brock hadn't asked Smith to do it, in fact he hadn't been pleased about it at all.

They had checked out the other ex-wives. One of them had moved out of state and had nothing good to say about him, though she denied any abuse. He had cheated on her.

The other one had also moved away after the divorce, and they'd learned she had passed away in an accident that didn't seem related.

Ex-wives. Children.

In each of the divorces, there had been a significant settlement, though Sarah was the only one who had wealth of her own. If John Smith had knowledge about the details, what was his role? She didn't think he had ever blackmailed Brock—in that case the latter wouldn't have hired him for a job.

How did someone go from wanting to win their former spouse back to trusting a criminal with hiding her and their daughter away until she changed her mind? Brock claimed he hadn't suspected anything. After all, he could see them every day, could see that the man brought them food and water—and while they weren't in luxurious surroundings, he didn't hold them in some kind of moldy basement either.

Luce laughed wryly. He'd said that as if thinking that would earn him any sympathy points with her.

A kidnapper for hire. He had to leave traces somewhere. They were going to find them.

❧

She went down to the lab to talk to Carrie Brayden again. Luce had little hope that John Smith was hiding Sarah and Poppy in one of Brock's properties. He had been genuinely upset to find that Smith had cut all ties—that had not been part of the plan.

"We are looking at every receipt and bank statement, for any pattern you told us to look out for. We are knee deep in them. This might take a while."

"I understand. Thank you anyway."

When she walked back to the elevator, her cell phone rang.

"Hey, Luce," her cousin Jill said. "I know you're probably at work, but I wanted to see how you're doing."

Genuine curiosity mixed in with the concern. Luce allowed herself a wry smile. They had always had that in common. Curiosity. It had sent them on different career paths. Here, Luce usually sent reporters to the communications department, happy to refer them to someone else.

Jill had cultivated close relationships with the detectives working on the cases she wrote about.

"I'm fine. I swear. But thank you. Everything okay over there? I'm pretty busy, but once this is over, I'd love for you and Josie to visit."

While her heart still ached for Kendra, finally introducing her to Jill was an exciting prospect.

"That would be great. Look, Luce, I know I'm treading a fine line, but is it possible to get a quote from you regarding Sarah Burke, how, or if this is related to the school bus kidnapping?"

"Wow," was all Luce could say.

"I'm really sorry. I shouldn't have…We'd love to come visit, if you'll still have us."

"No, that's okay. There's not a lot I can tell you at this moment. I'm just surprised this drew circles this wide."

"Well, Brock Construction is involved. Lots of money, the occasional transgression, messy divorces. I've heard a few stories."

"You have? Tell me more."

"Probably nothing you don't already know, but I've written a few articles about him and his business dealings."

"I'm looking for a John Smith, so that sounds better and better. Do you know if your friends with the PD have ever looked into the company?"

"I don't know, but I can always ask."

"Okay. That would be great. Off the record…" It was still amazing to her that Jill, two states away, was aware of the story beyond a few tidbits that might have made it to national news.

"Absolutely. I promise."

"Good. Brock paid someone to kidnap Burke and their daughter, but the deal was he'd never know their location. They'd be set free at some point once Sarah was willing to come back to him. He had access to a daily feed as proof that they were all right."

"That is messed up," Jill commented.

"It sure is, especially since there's no more feed, and no way to contact John Smith. We are trying to figure out who might have had an interest in doing Brock that kind of favor, and where they are now. One accomplice is still in the hospital after Smith shot him, the other one is on the lam."

The silence stretched on for several seconds.

"You've got your work cut out for you," Jill said. "Anything of that I can write?"

"I don't want Smith to know that Brock gave him up. That's too dangerous for Sarah and Poppy. Let's keep their pictures out there for the time being, and you can always contact our communications department. We have a sketch for the other guy, though I doubt he's somewhere near you."

She could swear Jill was smiling when she said, "So, that's how you want to play it. I ask you nicely for a favor and end up doing you a favor."

Luce couldn't help laughing. "Say hello to Josie. I miss her."

"I sure will. And we're going to meet your girlfriend next time?"

"She's eager to meet you two. We'll plan something soon."

"Great. I'll get back to you as soon as I know more."

"Thanks. And I'm sorry. If there's anything I can share, I'll let you know."

⌘

"Let's go over this again," Ritter said calmly. Luce appreciated him for it, because all she wanted to do was shake Brock. He had no interest in helping them finding evidence for crimes like fraud and tax evasion, but he had opinions.

"You haven't found Poppy yet? What kind of keystone cops are you?"

She remembered how he had never shown any concern for the children on the bus. Or Sarah. She assumed he didn't care that much about his own daughter either, beyond thinking of her as an asset. It made her sick to her stomach. And at times he reminded her so much of Hyde that she felt guilty for not figuring out the rest of the puzzle. She knew men like him, after all—didn't she?

Yet, there they were again, going around in circles.

"I told you, he contacted me. You know that already."

117

"And you put the fate of a woman and her child into the hands of a man who conveniently offered to abduct them for you? Right." Luce snorted.

"She's my child too, remember? And I don't think being alone with Sarah all the time was good for her. I noticed when I dropped off gifts. She was turning her against me. It was supposed to be safe!"

Ritter's expression was impassive, but for a split-second, Luce had seen a flash of disgusted disbelief.

"And you swear this is not a former employee of yours, someone you've hired for any sorts of jobs before?"

"We've been over this. I can't say for sure he didn't work for me before. If you're trying to catch me in a lie, forget about it."

"But why?"

Luce bit her lip to remind herself to keep her voice down. "How did you even imagine this would convince Sarah to come back? I understand you think you own her, but even considering that, it's at best delusional."

The disdain in his gaze was a dead giveaway as to what he was thinking. Predictable. He thought of himself as a player in a different world, a world someone like her would never understand. *Sheep, snowflake, bleeding heart.* Liberal. Luce had heard it all before.

"You might think of it as delusional. I wanted to keep my family together. Sarah was about to destroy it."

"So, you choose to intimidate and bully her into returning to a marriage she was unhappy in."

"Bully." He scoffed. "Such a mature choice of words, Detective."

"Why her? Why Sarah and not your other ex-wives? You had children with all of them. What made Sarah so special?"

Even as she kept talking, Luce was aware of the chill gripping her, of a possibility that was even more devious than what they already knew. The detective at the police department that had investigated the first wife's death found no evidence of foul play. The second wife denied abuse. Both had gotten settlements, like Sarah.

Sarah Burke was the only one with her own money.

Perhaps the plan was never to get her back, at least not for long.

"Mr. Brock, do you, or did you ever have access to Ms. Burke's accounts?"

She could tell from his face reddening with anger that he didn't like this line of questioning.

"What does that have to do with anything?"

"You never really cared what happened to Sarah, did you? I wonder if, when we're done going through your finances, we'll find an old insurance policy, or some proof that Sarah still has investments in your company, and you want to keep it that way. Maybe you owe her money..."

"I didn't want him to kill the bitch," he yelled, loudly enough for the officer in the corner to step closer. Luce shook her head.

"Tell us everything you know. We will get Poppy home—and Sarah, even if you don't care."

"Regardless of what you think, she cheated on me first. And I can't have that."

She could swear Ritter was trying not to roll his eyes.

"Let's go over this again. When did John Smith contact you? What exactly did he say?"

Chapter Fifteen

L uce sat on her couch with a soda and a bag of chips, vaguely thinking that she needed to make better choices. She wanted to, but at the moment, there was a chasm between good intentions and reality.

Brock swore that John Smith contacted him, that he implied they had friends in common, and Smith wanted to help out a friend in exchange for a reasonable sum.

Luce couldn't help thinking that this was either stupid, or naïve, or both. He had paid the biggest part upfront, cryptocurrency, impossible to trace. The rest...She doubted John Smith would stick around to collect it.

Something still didn't add up.

She put her notes aside and glanced at her phone. After a moment of hesitation, she texted Kendra.

How are you?

Okay, the answer came after a few seconds. *My colleagues have been amazing.*

That's good.

In the aftermath of traumatic events, the atmosphere and dynamics had improved in her own workplace. Ironically, Tyler becoming a permanent member of the team had changed said dynamics as well. He and Ritter had become friends, and Ritter had been more open to the occasional conversation. Luce had learned more about him and his family in the past month than she had in years working with him.

How's the case going? Kendra asked.

That was a good question. *It's going…somewhere*, she typed. *We have to get this done soon. Jill tells me it's getting attention at home. BTW, she'd love to meet you.*

Same here. When do we make it happen?

Luce couldn't help thinking something might be lost between the lines. She stared at the small screen for several seconds, working up the courage…Strange that she still hesitated to put it in words, after everything. But this was still so new, hopeful, precious…unlike pretty much the rest of the world. She cast a rueful glance at the bag of chips.

Soon, she wrote. *First, I'd like to see you.*

I'd like that too. No hesitation. *Work will be crazy, but would you like to sleep over tomorrow night? Like old times.*

Sleep over, yes, I'd love to. Not exactly like old times.

Kendra sent a smiling emoji and a heart.

I'm sorry, I need to get some sleep. Have a good night. Love you.

Love you too, Luce returned, only a few seconds later alerted by her rapid heartbeat of what had just happened.

It was only a logical step. Being around Kendra had always put her at ease in a way no one else made her feel. Kendra made her happy.

But she still had a job to do, and until it was done, that hint of guilt would always remain.

They were the same, which made things easier and more complicated at the same time.

Neither of them could forget completely.

A few hours later, the phone woke her from a surprisingly restful sleep.

"Good morning," she said, suppressing a yawn.

"It might be," Jill returned, sounding excited and a lot more awake than Luce. "Have you made any progress?"

Luce reasoned that she wouldn't call at this time just to ask her that. "I'm thinking that we need to look at Sarah more than we have so far. Yes, Brock has been pulling the strings, but there has to be more. I don't think she has done anything illegal, but something put her on John Smith's radar."

"You think the whole thing is about John Smith getting back at her for something? Interesting."

"That's all you have to say?"

"Actually, no. Have you looked into Brock's political contributions?"

"Some," Luce admitted. "It's a freaking cornucopia of information, which in this case, believe me, is not a good thing."

"I can imagine."

"His favorite candidates are usually right-wing, so-called traditional family values-types," she remembered. "Predictable, nothing much that stands out."

Did that mean anything anymore? Jared Hyde had run for State Senate, and his chances had been good until it turned out he had abducted women to keep them from having an abortion. One woman had died trying to escape, another had suffered a miscarriage.

Luce...He wanted to punish her after the fact, in his words, because he was called to do so. In Luce's words, because he was a criminal asshole who thought women owed him.

Her cousin, a single mother, had certainly encountered her not so fair share of that attitude.

"I came across a story from a few years ago," Jill continued. "Brock was still married to Sarah Burke back then, and he was backing the candidate on the far right. The more moderate conservative dropped out after a scandal involving sex workers, so…it was the extreme guy, and his opponent. The latter had an accident, and Brock's favorite won."

"That's a bit far-fetched," Luce said. "You don't think Brock had his hands in that?" She left her bedroom and walked into the kitchen where she put Jill on speaker and started preparing the coffee she desperately needed at this point.

"Not sure," Jill admitted. "What I did find out was that the winning candidate had some sort of fixer. He was suspected of setting up the moderate conservative and having a hand in the accident, though they couldn't prove it. I raised a touchy subject. Everyone's still pissed about that."

"I can imagine. Where is that fixer now?"

Luce had her first sip of coffee, and it tasted magical. Like progress. Like hope.

"No one knows. He disappeared off the face of the Earth."

"Jill, you are the best. I'll definitely look into this, and I might give Harding a call."

"She wasn't a detective back then. The detective on the case, Waters, is retired, but I'm sure Maria Doss will talk to you. I can ask her."

"That's great. Thank you so much. Could you email me what you have on this, names of everyone involved? I swear you'll be the first to know if this goes anywhere."

"Hope springs eternal." Jill laughed. "It's okay. I'm happy to help."

"I'll make it up to you," Luce promised. "Kendra is looking forward to meeting you. We'll do it soon."

"Definitely. Have a great day, Luce."

"You too."

Luce had planned to have a semi-healthy breakfast at home, but she couldn't wait to get to the station. She put some coffee in a travel mug and grabbed a muffin from the fridge. That would do.

Before the briefing, she had made a detour to the lab, hoping to get some numbers to back up her new findings. What Carrie provided her with seemed promising. So, Luce was excited to share with her colleagues and D.A. Troy who, to no surprise, voiced doubts.

"Are you sure about this?" she asked. "We can't always make this about politics. At some point, people will take notice and wonder if we're really objective in this."

"At this point, we're not accusing anyone else." Luce was proud of herself for keeping her voice calm. She could see Chomsky's small smile, a reaction she probably deserved after going off on Troy not that long ago. For Sarah and Poppy's sake, she was determined to keep their differences out of the workplace, though it wasn't always easy. Sometimes, in her opinion, Troy's biases affected the work. She couldn't dwell on that now.

"Here's the connection: Brock invested substantially in that race, enough for the candidate to be aware, and to want to cultivate him as a donor. Ted Dobbs is running again, though his chances aren't as good this time around. Back in the days, he had someone people thought to be his fixer, a man called Bobby Milano. Milano was suspected of framing one candidate and putting another one in the hospital."

"That sounds like political fiction," Troy mumbled.

"I think it sounds intriguing," Tyler disagreed, "but aside from the donation, what's the connection to Brock? You really think Bobby Milano is John Smith?"

"He was supposed to come in for an interview, vanished before they could pick him up, and was never seen again. He seems like the type who could pull off something like, let's say, kidnap an entire school bus. The way he went at Wheeler, it fits. Obviously, he has lots of connections, people who owe him."

"That candidate, Dobbs, he could be the mutual friend," Ritter mused.

If the situation wasn't so serious, Luce would have taken a moment to be astonished. She'd never felt like she'd gotten this much support from her colleagues before. Chomsky did the best she could, but she had to keep politics in mind.

"I've been talking to Brayden, and my source can get me more as well. I am sure it's Bobby Milano we are looking for. That," she couldn't help it, "has nothing to do with politics, though Dobbs has done considerable damage since he was elected."

Chomsky's gaze held a hint of both amusement and warning.

"Regardless, it's not him we're going to arrest."

"Much as some of you'd like to." Apparently, Troy thought two could play that game. "This sounds like a lead to follow," she said, getting to her feet. "All right. Let me know when you know more."

"Will do, Counselor."

Chapter Sixteen

"You enjoyed that quite a bit," Tyler mumbled when they got back to their desks.

Luce couldn't help smiling. "I did. But it doesn't matter. We have a chance now."

"True, but it won't be easy," he reminded her. "We won't be the first interested in talking to Milano, and so far, he has done a pretty good job of hiding from the authorities."

"If he really is John Smith, there are people he's interacted with lately. People he has pissed off. He can't hide forever."

"From your mouth to God's ears," he said before settling behind his own desk.

"You're quite the pessimist today. Everything all right?"

"Yeah, I'm fine. You are the one who's unusually optimistic." Before Luce could answer, he made a dismissive gesture. "I'm not arguing. It is a lead. The sooner this guy is behind bars, the better."

Luce went back to the material Jill had sent her, about the candidates, the mysterious Bobby Milano. In every picture with Dobbs, he was wearing sunglasses, and it was hard to tell if he was the same man Justin had seen, who had shot Wheeler...but it could be. Height, body type, hair, all if it seemed about right.

Jill had added photos from fundraisers and other functions, a couple of them showing Brock and his then wife, Sarah, at an event with the moderate candidate who was later ousted because of the scandal. The story was somewhat remarkable, as these days a scandal like this wouldn't topple a candidate who had the "right" lines.

Luce wondered if Sarah had been aligned with any of the ones running, or if Brock forced her to attend.

According to Brock and Layne, she was financially independent. A look into her finances would be interesting as well. Luce looked over to Chomsky's office, but Troy, who had joined her after the briefing, was already gone.

Of course, now they had to focus on Milano first.

A few phone calls were in order.

Brock, to no one's surprise, denied that he had ever met Milano in person. Layne claimed that he and Sarah hadn't discussed politics, or her marriage with Brock, a lot, though according to him, she'd often say more women were needed in positions of power.

Amen, Luce thought when she hung up the phone.

Maria Doss, the detective Jill had referred her to, sounded tired and frustrated, but she was willing to reminisce.

"Jill told me you might call," she said. "Milano…There have been some sightings over the years, but nothing in the past two. For all we know, he may be dead. No record anywhere that I'm aware of though, so I assume he used the global chaos during the pandemic to stay hidden. I'm sorry I can't help you more."

"That's okay. Thank you for making the time. Just one more thing—could you tell me if you looked at the donors at the time? Mr. Brock, his wife maybe?"

"Not really. We were aware that some withdrew donations when they realized their guy might not have played fair. Well, I don't think they cared that much, but they didn't want to be associated with the appearance of impropriety. You know what I mean."

"Yeah. Again, thank you."

"Anything I can do to help," the detective said grimly. "I remember that case, and even if we couldn't prove it was him...the guy is violent. This went far beyond destroying reputations. He put a woman in a wheelchair."

"Francine Kendrick."

"Exactly. Guess what, she's running against Dobbs again. That takes some guts."

"Definitely."

Luce spent the next few hours trying to put the pieces together. Was Dobbs more careful this time? Had he hired a different fixer? Or was he keeping in touch with his former, seemingly loyal employee?

But where was the connection to Sarah?

She was none the wiser regarding those questions when she arrived at Kendra's house that night, after stopping at her own home to take a shower and pack an overnight bag. Perhaps they could take a few days off, sometime in the future, and get out of the city? That seemed like a faraway dream at the moment, but one she wanted to hold on to.

They both needed it. Neither of them had stopped much in the past few years outside of sick leave.

The fantasy was still on her mind when Kendra opened the door to her, dressed in skinny jeans and a shiny top that made Luce feel underdressed—though she was happy to see that Kendra seemed to feel better.

"I didn't know you wanted to go out," she said. "I would have gone with something more appropriate." She tugged at her t-shirt.

"Don't worry. I didn't plan on going out...and you look perfect."

"That's a strong word..." Luce started, though she couldn't deny the compliment warmed her. "How have you been doing?"

Kendra's smile faltered a little. She straightened.

"It wasn't the first time something like that happened. Sadly, it won't be the last, and I'm afraid it will only get worse. I grieve for her. At the same time, I refuse to give in to fear. I know we can't save everyone, much as we wish. I believe the best way to honor them is to continue the work, and to live our lives. Proudly so."

"I agree." Luce reached out to brush her fingers over her cheek and tuck a strand of her behind her ear. "I'm so glad you're in mine."

"Me too. You've made a big difference...Aside from arresting the guy who wanted to blow up my workplace."

That made her flinch, but she couldn't deny it was the truth.

"So, I hope you don't mind me asking, but what is for dinner?"

That made Kendra laugh. "You're insatiable."

Just like that, in a heartbeat, the atmosphere shifted, nearly making her dizzy with the jolt of emotion and desire. How could she have ignored this between them for so long? Perhaps denial was the better term.

"You know me, I'm always hungry," she said, placing a soft kiss on Kendra's lips, the contact causing a delightful shiver. Her, Kendra, she wasn't even sure.

"Don't worry. I'm going to take care of all your needs. Let's eat first?"

All of it sounded heavenly. Perhaps a bit of that good life could happen even while they kept doing the job.

She stood in the bedroom later, a space where she had spent many nights after long conversations, a safe space where she could leave all her rage at the world, all her fears of an ever-worsening future behind. Because Kendra dealt with the same reality, and she never seemed that afraid.

It was still safe, but in a new and exciting way.

Luce smiled as Kendra's arms came around her, and curious hands stole underneath her shirt, skimming over her ribs softly enough to tickle. It wasn't what made her gasp though, but the brush of fingertips over the fabric of her bra, making her warm and tingly all over with anticipation.

"I promised you."

"And I never had any doubts." She turned around before those curious hands could reach the waistband of her jeans and pulled Kendra close to her, initiating a deep breathless kiss. They undressed each other with quick impatient moves until they made it to the bed. With Kendra's body warm and pliant underneath her, Luce wasn't going to stop to turn off any lights.

Focusing on the feel of warm skin against her own, that ever-present voice of doubt was finally silent.

Bobby Milano had dropped off the face of the Earth a few years ago as Jill had told her, but his influence loomed large. There was no time to dive into details of the old campaign, but Luce had learned enough to understand that the reputation of Dobbs' moderate challenger had never recovered. He had left politics but given the occasional interview where he kept pointing out how unfair things had been—these days, no one would get ousted over paying off sex workers for kinky services rendered.

Luce had to admit that the man had a point, though she thought that Milano had gone easier on him. Before he became the victim of a set-up cleverly orchestrated by Milano, he had spent quite some time in seedy hotel rooms cheating on his wife.

The woman, Francine Kendrick who was challenging the incumbent Dobbs, had gone through extensive surgeries and therapy to be where she was now, mounting another campaign with the support of her family and most of her old team. Even a quick glance had shown Luce the vitriol she'd been subjected to online, not that it came as any surprise.

All of that was on the backburner for now, finding Bobby Milano the priority. The needle in the haystack.

As another day came to a close, she sat in front of her computer, wiping a tired hand over her face. They had to start thinking about the unthinkable. Finding the children from the bus, returning them to their parents had been such a high.

Now they had to prepare for the worst, because what would be Bobby Milano's motivation to keep Sarah and Poppy alive if he couldn't extort money from Brock?

Her stomach turned at the possibilities.

"I'm calling it a day," she said quietly. Tyler looked up as she passed by his desk.

"Want to grab dinner?"

Just two colleagues hanging out together. Now that the air was clear between them, it could have been an option, but Luce had something else on her mind.

"No thanks. I think I'll stop by Sarah's on the way."

He leaned back in his chair, studying her. "What are you hoping to find there that none of us found the first time...or the other times?"

"I don't know," she admitted with a shrug. "It's just frustrating. We move forward an inch and then hit a wall again. How the hell could he stay under the radar for this long?"

"Friends in high places?" Tyler mused. "Or really low, depending on your perspective, I guess. I hear you though. John and I will go to Mike's if you change your mind."

Kendra was working late this week. All of a sudden, the deep-fried, definitely not-what-the-doctor-ordered, food of Mike's sounded heavenly.

"I might," she said. "Otherwise, have a good night."

"You too."

He was right, Luce thought when she let herself into the dark house. She turned on the lights and walked around the same rooms she and her colleagues had examined already, nothing more to find, no sudden revelation. The same sad scenario. Milano had walked in on Sarah and Poppy making breakfast and taken them someplace where a constant camera feed was supposed to reassure Brock. She shook her head even though there was no one around.

Men like that had nothing if they didn't use money and intimidation.

"Sad," she said out loud. Her gaze fell once again on the pictures on the mantel. Mostly of Poppy, alone or with Sarah, and with an older couple she knew to be her parents. Both were deceased.

Her throat grew tight as she imagined it might be too late for mother and daughter.

"Give me something, damn it."

Once again, she opened drawers and cabinets. Sarah had a few folders with papers relating to banking and insurance policies, but the rest was likely all digital, like for most people. The kidnapper had taken her electronics.

That included any recent photos. She remembered Matt Layne saying that they were careful when it came to social media. Sarah didn't have much of an online footprint, just an account where she mostly gathered links and videos to crafts and recipes. And cat videos. Luce assumed that most of it was for Poppy.

What had put Sarah on Milano's radar?

Or even Brock's, before? Yes, her parents had been wealthy, but they didn't seem to have walked in the same circles as someone like him.

Luce picked up a photo album, leafing through it absent-mindedly. Poppy was still a baby back then. She chose another volume, this one showing family and friends, with Poppy about four years old—around the time Brock had given his support to Ted Dobbs.

He was in very few of the photos, even though they were still married back then. Luce closed the album with a sigh, not getting anything new. There was one more, and she decided to wrap up her wild goose chase after this in favor of one of Mike's signature burgers.

This one showed Sarah as a younger woman, before Poppy was born. Some parties, the group photo of a basketball team. Luce scanned the faces, all of a sudden excited. She might be getting desperate, but...

There it was. She picked up her phone and did a quick search until she found what she was looking for. Francine Kendrick, around the same age. Not the same picture, but it was clear that she had been one of the team members.

Brock's actions were definitely those of a jealous possessive stalker, but had politics played a part in the couple's failed marriage?

Luce went back to the living room where she pulled out a folder that held actual papers. Back then, or recently, had Sarah contributed to Francine's campaign? Jealousy, political disputes, or both?

Luce decided to give Francine Kendrick a call tomorrow. She went through all the rooms again to make sure the lights were off. She realized she had forgotten one downstairs where the laundry room was located. Back on the stairs to the ground floor, she heard the clicking sound. It was enough to accelerate her heart rate. Door in the lock? A gun? None of those were good.

Since her return to work, she had been cautious. Coming here for a quick check shouldn't have been a risk given that the man they were looking for had an interest in staying under the radar. Abduction. Attempted murder. Worst case scenario, murder.

Would he send Wheeler's accomplice, the man who had hit Caitlyn?

Get a grip. Perhaps Tyler had decided to check up on her. He wasn't the patronizing type, but he might have thought of something as well.

Luce took another step, careful not to make any noise. She heard footsteps. There was definitely someone in the house, but if it had been Tyler, he would have called out by now. She picked up her phone and clicked 911, hand on her weapon. While on the phone with the dispatcher, she could hear the intruder walk around. She could probably make it back downstairs and out the back, wait for her colleagues.

She could feel her palms go sweaty, her heart hammering by now. An intruder had surprised her in her home one time, when the renovations were still underway. So many things had been in motion. After her abduction, she had worked hard to feel safe again, at all, not just at the house...Whatever she had achieved, Luce could feel it crumble.

She drew her firearm as she slowly retreated. She could still hear the heavy footsteps on the floor above as she made it back down to the basement and to the back door. One step at a time. Within minutes, her colleagues would be here.

Was she doing the right thing, or wasting precious time? She should be making that arrest. If Bobby Milano was upstairs, he wouldn't stay for long, and he'd certainly bolt if he saw squad cars outside.

This was her job, damn it. She could surprise him.

Most of all, she shouldn't be standing here imagining all the worst-case scenarios.

Luce opened the door leading out to the backyard, determined to meet her backup out front. If Milano wanted to bolt, she was going to keep him from doing so.

Sarah and Poppy had to be alive. They had to be.

She took one step outside to have her world explode with pain the next moment.

Luce staggered back, tasting blood. She reached for the wall behind her, the brick scraping her palm as she failed. The side of her face was on fire with the agony, but she could see the man walking away. He was fucking whistling.

She managed to get a hold of the gun she had dropped when he hit her and point it in a shaky hand. She pulled the trigger.

Sirens.

And then, nothing.

The last image was of the wooden two-by-four next to her, with red on it.

Chapter Seventeen

Jill had made dinner for herself and Josie, and after a bit of TV, put her daughter to bed. The process was longer now that Josie's opinions on bedtime rituals were changing. More and more she wanted to stay up, worried about what she might miss, wondering about what Jill was doing.

Normally, Jill didn't mind, but today she sighed in relief when Josie was asleep, and she picked up her phone. In her office, pictures were strewn all over her desk.

After speaking to Maria Doss, she had dug deeper into the story of Ted Dobbs bypassing all challengers with means that might not have been entirely legal. Back in the day, no one had paid much attention to Brock and his then wife Sarah, but they had been in many headlines lately, and a lot of people were starting to wonder what connected all these stories...or better, who.

Bobby Milano.

She picked up her phone and chose Luce's number once again. She quite liked that they were talking more, not exactly the events that had led to it. Working closely with the local department in the past few years, she had gotten a taste of what the job could look like.

She hadn't thought about it too much when she and Luce used to exchange phone calls every few months, and Luce rarely talked about work. Until it all caught up with them.

Why was she thinking of this now?

When Luce didn't pick up after three rings, Jill resigned to the fact that she'd have to leave a voicemail—but before the recorded message came on, her call was answered.

"Hello? This is Kendra."

Jill immediately understood that Luce's girlfriend picking up the phone wasn't random.

"Is Luce okay?" she asked, alarmed. "I'm Jill. Her cousin."

"Jill." She sounded tired. There was something else to her tone, something that scared Jill. She knew before Kendra said, "She'll be okay. I promise." No one would say anything like that if they didn't have bad news to pair it with. Jill braced herself.

❧

She hadn't been out that long, and learned with some satisfaction that Bobby Milano, too, had left blood all over the scene. Other than that, Luce didn't have much to be satisfied with. She wanted to be anywhere but in this hospital room.

She could still taste blood, the combination with the smells of the hospital making her stomach turn even though she was hungry. Not a surprise since she'd never gotten to that juicy burger.

She hurt all over, but the inferno still centered around the left side of her face where Milano had hit her with the two-by-four. Her tongue went to the stitches inside her mouth even though she remembered the doctor advising her to avoid exactly that.

A few more visible ones as well—She hadn't dared look into a mirror yet.

The impact had broken at least one tooth, which meant she was in for more pain, and as far as she knew, Sarah and Poppy were still missing. Damn it all.

He could have shot her, so all things considered, she might be lucky. Luce didn't feel that way, especially when Kendra came through the door.

Just imagining what she had to look like, paired with tonight's failure, made sure Kendra was the last person she wanted to see right now.

"Luce."

The way Kendra said her name revealed all her emotions at once, too much for her composure.

Luce simply shook her head, afraid she'd embarrass herself further if she tried to speak. This night was already going to Hell.

"You don't have to be here," she managed. "I don't want you to...See..."

"Come on," Kendra said softly. "It was horrible having to wait out there, but at least they talked to me. I got hold of a friend who owes me a favor, and he will see you to get your teeth fixed as soon as they let you out of here."

Luce winced. "Teeth?"

"A couple. I'm so sorry, baby. But I hear you were badass and shot the asshole."

Even though part of her face was numb, there was still a pounding ache, which made it hard to focus. But she was pretty sure Kendra had called her baby, and badass in the same sentence. She would have smiled if she hadn't been afraid of drooling.

"Lucky," she said with a shrug, and winced again. "Fuck."

"I know." Kendra carefully took her hand, one of the few parts of her body that didn't hurt. Luce closed her eyes at the gentle touch.

"He got away though. I should have never..." She shook her head. So many things. Not go alone to the house. Confront him before he had the chance to slam a piece of wood in her face.

"You did everything you could," Kendra protested, as if she knew what she was talking about. "Ritter, Murphy and Chomsky are still here as well, but when I played the doctor *and* girlfriend card, everyone agreed it was my turn."

Almost unreal that the last time they'd met, Luce had put on a hint of make-up, something she rarely did, dressed for a date...felt sexy.

This was about as far from sexy as anyone could be, and she still wished she could have cleaned up more before seeing her. At the very least, she wouldn't give in to misery and start sobbing with her colleagues just outside the door.

"Thank you," she whispered, and leaned into Kendra who embraced her carefully.

"You are so welcome."

Tyler came in a few minutes later, fortunately after she had pulled herself together enough to have a semi-professional conversation. Kendra's quiet, calm way of dealing with the situation was a relief, yet, Luce hoped there would be a day, sometime soon, when she wouldn't lean on her so hard.

It wasn't something she was used to, and it troubled her. There was no time to investigate any reasons irrational or justified, and she liked that just fine.

"Ouch," he said, sympathetic.

"That about covers it," she mumbled. "Any news on Milano?"

He shook his head. "Word is out. He's injured. He can't get that far."

"I should have taken him in. We would know what happened to Sarah and Poppy by now."

"We will soon. The most important thing is for you to get back on your feet again, but I'm not worried, since you have a doctor at your service..."

Luce might have appreciated his attempt to have her look on the bright side, but his words illuminated her problem with the circumstances. They also triggered a memory that was highly inappropriate in this context—even though it made everything hurt a little less.

"Yeah, right. I can't complain."

"I wasn't saying that. If I were you, I'd complain plenty. Poor Luce. There will be a good amount of mushy food in your near future."

Luce groaned. With her body still in chaos, she hadn't thought of that at all.

"Chomsky will want me to take time off." She didn't mean for it to sound petulant. Luce was more than aware she wasn't going back to work tomorrow, and once she got to go home...She had a date with Kendra's friend, the dentist. Her tongue went back to the sharp edge of the broken tooth.

"Have you looked into a mirror?" Tyler asked in disbelief.

"Wow, thanks."

"I think you should get some rest now," he reasoned.

"If you find anything, let me know, and don't take all the credit."

"We'll see...I'm kidding! Take the time you need. I'm serious." He patted her shoulder and turned to leave.

"I really wanted that burger." He gave her a sympathetic look before he stepped aside to let Lieutenant Chomsky into the room and then left.

Insult to injury, Luce thought. Someone else would find Milano and rightfully so, take the credit. It shouldn't matter to her at all. It didn't matter as long as Sarah and Poppy were alive. Something sprang to mind, and she wanted to slap her hand against her forehead—maybe she would have, but she didn't care for adding any more pain.

"He was there for the same thing," she said, her self-consciousness rising to new levels in front of Chomsky who was her usual put-together self. In addition to her scary looks, Luce sounded off, slightly slurring the words because of the local anesthesia. At the moment, she didn't care. "I was going to call Ms. Kendrick. I think this has something to do with donations Sarah made to her campaign. Neither Brock nor Milano wanted her to win, then and now. I was going to ask her to come in."

"I can do that," Chomsky offered. "We found the papers where you left them. Milano never got to them."

That was a relief at least.

"I believe she might be able to shed some light on this."

"It will be okay. I believe Detective Murphy promised you updates, but I don't want to see you at the station before Monday, you hear me?"

Chomsky rarely raised her voice. She didn't need to.

Luce nodded.

"I'm glad we have an understanding, but even more so to know you'll be all right. This is someone who shot an accomplice point blank."

She didn't care for being reminded. It didn't mean good things for the woman and child still missing.

"I was waiting for back-up."

"I understand. That wasn't a criticism. I have to get back to the office...I know you don't feel great right now, but we're making lots of progress because you put the pieces together. I hope you remember that."

"Yeah, right," Luce muttered, but not before Chomsky had left the room.

Kendra returned at the same time, catching her antics.

"Did I just see you make a face at your supervisor?" Her soft tone held amusement.

"She deserved it. Look...I'm really tired, and I'm sure you've had a long day as well. Why don't we talk tomorrow?"

"I'm good," Kendra said. "I had something to eat and a coffee."

"Coffee." Luce winced at her tone that sounded both whiny and jealous to her.

"But I brought you this." Kendra held up a beverage from a nearby coffee shop. "I know you're going to need something soft and not too hot, and I promise you, this is delicious."

"Thank you," she said, taking the cup with the straw in it.

If she had to be careful for the next few days, an indulgent chocolate banana smoothie wasn't the worst choice.

"It's good," she admitted after the first sip. "There is something different about it though..."

"It's the tofu," Kendra explained.

"Really?"

"Yes, really. It's for the protein." She laughed when she realized Luce was yanking her chain. "Come on."

The light moment had come and gone too soon. Kendra was making herself comfortable in the visitor's chair, as much as that was possible.

Luce was too exhausted to argue. She didn't consider it possible, but when she lay back down, still wound up with embarrassment, frustration and the faint hope that all of this wasn't for nothing...She was asleep within minutes.

It was a restless night interwoven with nightmares. Luce hated to wake up crying. It had happened more than she would have liked to admit in the past weeks, and she wanted to be done. She didn't want anyone to witness it, least of all Kendra, but she couldn't deny that the cool gentle touch to her face was so very welcome.

Chapter Eighteen

D espite the promises, Luce didn't hear much from her colleagues for two days, except for a short text from Tyler telling her that they hadn't found Milano yet. Ritter dropped by and offered her a ride to the clinic where Kendra's friend had secured an appointment for her. She took him up on it, eager to get the dental work out of the way.

Kendra picked Luce up afterwards to drive her home so she could pick up a few clothes.

"I promise, this was the hardest part. You'll be fine," she said when Luce got into the car.

"I definitely don't look fine...but I guess I'll live." The stitches were still in place, and the headache reminded her of the other work done in her mouth.

"You definitely will."

Kendra kissed her lips very softly, and she shrank back, thinking she had to taste like every product the dentist had used.

"Did I hurt you?"

"No. No, it's just...a lot," Luce said vaguely for the lack of better words.

"I know. Let's go home, and make something to eat?"

It seemed like lately, that was their solution to everything.

Kendra was doing her best to give her space while Luce, in the temporary absence of a day job, remained in a state of confusion, wanting her close, wanting her at a distance until she felt more like herself again.

But had she, at any point, since the car crash and subsequent events?

Everything they had shared since then seemed like a dream, too good to be true or withstand the reality of their jobs. Not that every cop in the city was cursed with as much bad luck as Luce had been lately—or maybe she just attracted a certain type of criminal.

Not in the mood to go back to her own house, she fired off a few texts in the hope for answers and perused some of Kendra's paperback novels.

Francine Kendrick confirmed receiving donations from Sarah Burke both times, Tyler replied after ten minutes. *Now eat your soup and take a nap.*

Easy for him to say.

Restless, Luce tossed the phone aside and went back to her novel. A few minutes later, she picked it up again and scrolled through the menu of a nearby restaurant. Chocolate cheesecake would meet her temporary needs.

It was delivered half an hour later and alleviated her restlessness and anxiety for at least a few minutes. No black coffee, because it was too hot.

No, this wasn't working.

Luce carefully brushed her teeth and wrote a note for Kendra, sent another text to Tyler, and left. Her car still sat outside the house from when Kendra had brought it over, anticipating that Luce would spend some time here. She sat behind the wheel, took a deep breath, and pulled out of the parking spot.

Her phone lit up with a message, but Luce chose to ignore it for the moment when she saw it was Jill. She couldn't take any more kind concern, not now.

⁂

Much to her relief, no one questioned her presence. Lieutenant Chomsky wasn't in her office, but Luce assumed she might hear a few words from her when she returned. Tyler was out too, but he had received her latest text. Before he left, he had put his notes, with everything they had on the connection between Sarah and Francine Kendrick, on her desk.

On a sticky note, he had written, *There you go. What happened to that nap?*

"Funny," she muttered.

Since there was no one there to chide her about it, Luce went and got herself a coffee from the breakroom.

Back at her desk, she settled in and started to read, suppressing a curse when the still hot beverage touched the wound. Waiting for it to cool down had not come as a habit yet.

Her reading material was interesting enough to distract her though: Sarah Burke had played on her college basketball team alongside Francine Kendrick. They weren't best friends, but later when Kendrick ran for office, Sarah had sent a substantial donation.

Luce brought up Kendrick's current website. Her campaign put a focus on anti-corruption and promised to protect citizens, especially vulnerable ones, from overreach of corporations, including banks, other loan businesses, and real estate developers.

It wasn't hard to see why Brock would root for the other guy who would jump at any opportunity to give these particular industries even more power—which, in return, would be good

147

for his business, fewer regulations, fewer permits to pay, more profit for Brock construction.

She didn't think they had the whole story yet.

Why would Sarah want to make a point? An overbearing jealous husband, an unhappy marriage might be enough of an explanation.

On the other hand, why was Milano so interested in her? He had shown considerable loyalty to his boss Dobbs, but there had to be many other donors. Why single out Sarah? Did he want to please Brock so badly, or did Dobbs? More checks for his attack ads, more money for his super PAC?

She suppressed a sigh. It was always good advice to follow the money. Jared Hyde's financial issues had been one of the first things to tip her off. She wasn't looking forward to dealing with another one of his kind.

I don't want to change minds, I want to change laws. She remembered those words clearly. Hyde was in prison. Ted Dobbs represented a district, where he was doing everything he could to trample on the rights of women and vulnerable communities.

She heard a door open. It wasn't Chomsky, but Troy who walked in, stopping cold when she saw Luce, which could be for a few reasons. She felt a little less self-conscious since her teeth had been fixed, but her face still showed proof of her encounter with the two-by-four. The memory made every muscle in her body spasm in protest.

"The lieutenant isn't in?" Troy asked, as if they couldn't both see right into the empty office.

"I don't know where she is, sorry. But since you're here, maybe you could give me your take on something."

"I'm intrigued."

Perhaps she deserved that, because she didn't usually start conversations with the D.A. like that. Most of the time, she knew what Liz Troy was thinking, and they rarely saw eye to eye.

"How much do you know about the Ted Dobbs affair?"

"Affair?" She raised an eyebrow. "I didn't know you were looking into him. I thought it was Milano that you wanted."

"We suspect Milano of having abducted Sarah and Poppy Burke, yes, but it seems that he was Dobbs's personal fixer. In your opinion, does that kind of loyalty go both ways?"

"In politics?" Troy gave a wry laugh, and Luce remembered that she, too, had aspirations to run for office. "As soon as Milano became a liability, he would have dropped him like a hot potato. But you know that. Why are you asking me?"

"It's what I thought, but you have more insight into these dynamics. Someone is lending Milano a hand. There's no way he could have stayed hidden for this long."

"Or someone is keeping him on a short leash," Troy said, pensive. "Look, in politics, both sides play dirty."

Luce suppressed a sigh.

"But that case got really ugly, and while we couldn't prove that Dobbs's campaign had anything to do with Kendrick's accident, it was a theory that made more sense than others."

"Dobbs got what he wanted, and as the incumbent, he's still leading in the polls, unbelievable as that is."

"It is," Troy agreed. "Brock isn't talking either." It wasn't a question. For the past few days, she had probably been more in the loop than Luce.

"It doesn't make sense. He claims that Milano approached him, yet they never met. Why this elaborate scheme?"

"Well, and here she is," Troy commented with regard to the lieutenant who had just walked in. "If you find the answer to that question, let me know."

"I'm sorry to keep you waiting," Chomsky said. "Let's go to my office. And good afternoon, Detective Allen."

Her tone left no doubt that she'd have more words for Luce later.

She had better find a good reason to still be here.

When Troy left about half an hour later, Chomsky stopped by Luce's desk.

"I know what you want to say, but I feel fine. Okay, that might be stretching it a bit, but I've taken a few days as you recommended. Something isn't sitting right with me. Brock thinks of his family as property, sure. They wanted to keep Sarah from supporting Kendrick, I think that's part of the issue. It's not quite coming together yet."

"Nice try." Chomsky shook her head. "I've told you before, it isn't that we don't appreciate your contribution, but wouldn't you agree everyone deserves a break at some point?"

I deserve a break when Sarah and Poppy are home safely. She didn't say it out loud, knowing it wouldn't be helpful. Besides, she had taken breaks in ways she wasn't going to discuss with the lieutenant.

"No argument from me. I just asked Murphy for his notes so I could bring myself up to date. I talked to D.A. Troy. I promise I'll go home in a bit."

"I was hoping you'd say that. Good afternoon, Lieutenant."

"Dr. Jones. It's good to see you again."

After the amiable greeting, Chomsky went back to her office. Kendra didn't waste any time.

"I promise I won't always randomly show up at your workplace, but I thought that while you're technically still on leave, it's a little less inappropriate."

Her state of mind was still in a precarious balance. She needed something to occupy her mind, but if she was honest, she hadn't achieved much here. Her face still hurt, though the pain pills managed to take the edge off.

"I don't want you to worry about me." That was about as honest as she could get.

"I know, and good luck with that." Kendra gave a self-conscious laugh. "On the other hand, I got off work early which almost never happens, and if you're up to it, we could have dinner somewhere. I know you get cabin fever quickly."

"I'm really sorry. You know I'm grateful for everything you've done. And I can leave here right now."

As they walked outside together, Luce realized to her surprise that she could breathe a little easier than she had been able to for the last few days. They were all right, of course. She needed to take some time, deal with what had happened. Everything. Luce also knew that the loose ends of this case would keep her mind occupied meanwhile.

Regardless, she would be back at work full time come Monday, and then early dinners would be an extremely rare thing again.

"I could go for Thai," she said.

"We'll find something that works for you," Kendra promised.

Chapter Nineteen

S he was right, as usual. The quiet ambience and excellent food helped. They found dishes on the menu appropriate for Luce's current condition, and she finally voiced what had been on her mind when she had all but fled to work earlier.

"I'm so sorry," she said. "You've been amazing, and I...I didn't mean to run away. It's just that I've been leaning on you a lot, and it made me feel like I wasn't pulling my weight."

"No. You came back from a traumatic experience, only to get hit in the face with...Sorry, I don't mean to remind you," Kendra returned, and they shared a smile.

"I guess those stitches will remind me for some days to come but thank you."

"You were there for me too," she continued. "I didn't want to call you, and then I hoped you might be psychic and realize how much I wanted you there..."

"I don't know about psychic, but I wanted to. I'm still so sorry it happened."

"I know." With a sigh, Kendra reached for her water glass. "And perhaps there are things I haven't told you, when I should have. You know, I didn't lie to you when I said I don't want to give the people protesting outside too much importance. I know we help far more than they can scare away. You and I deal in different ways, and that's okay, but after what happened I couldn't keep it at a distance anymore. I was so afraid for you."

Technically, Luce had known that. Their mutual admissions had come at a difficult time, and the only reason they had made it through the darkest parts was that those feelings had existed pretty much from the start.

Not that she could hold anyone responsible but herself, but her brief fling with Tyler had happened at a time of deep and oppressive loneliness. She hadn't felt close to anyone in her life except Kendra—but Kendra wasn't interested in more than friendship. At least that's what Luce had told herself back then. She had also told herself that it would be better that way, less complicated. How wrong she had been.

They were still navigating their changed relationship between hope and reality. It had transformed everything, even them.

"I know." She wouldn't ever want to be in that position, but Luce understood a whole lot more about the recent dynamics. "I promise you, it won't always be like that. Sometimes it's just interviews and paperwork for long stretches of time."

Wordlessly, Kendra reached out to take her hand. For some reason, the innocent, tender gesture made her heartbeat go into overdrive.

Luce remembered that moment later when they lay in bed together, close, how she had almost suggested that her house could become rental property someday. She snuggled into the warmth of Kendra's body. She'd never felt as safe anywhere as she did here.

⁂

"Are you okay up there?"

They had gone to Luce's house once more where she packed a few more things, and the thought of renting it out to a stranger became even more attractive.

When she was attacked in her home, it happened downstairs, and the worst thing the intruder had done was to vandalize drywall. No comparison. Nothing bad had happened here afterwards, yet she sat on the side of the tub in her upstairs bathroom, shivering as her shirt stuck to her skin. Struggling to breathe, she gripped the edge of the tub with both hands.

"I'll be right down," she called and finally got to her feet. This had to stop. She changed into a new shirt, tossed the other one into the hamper and went downstairs where Kendra was waiting for her.

She had promised her better times. Luce wasn't going to let her down. And once those stitches were gone, she would hopefully stop obsessing about something that was in the past.

"Let's go."

It seemed obscene to go take a walk in the park given the state of the case, but Luce had to accept she wasn't irreplaceable. And when she would get back to work, her colleagues would need to rely on her one hundred percent. This morning's episode had her worried, but she still had some time until Monday.

⁂

They spent Sunday night at Luce's place. She didn't have another flashback, but she had come to some sobering conclusions after she and Kendra had talked. Both were used to being in control, both had wanted to put recent events behind them as soon as possible.

But some of these processes were outside their control.

Luce remembered the therapist's warning when she told her with conviction that she was fine and just wanted to get on with her life.

Hell, the 24/7 news cycle was full of triggers, not to mention her job. But like she'd told Kendra, it wouldn't always be that way.

Calmer waters had to be ahead somewhere, didn't they?

She might be getting ahead of herself, but she'd still love to wake up next to Kendra every day. Not to waste any more time. It hadn't gone well for Sarah Burke and Matt Layne.

Monday morning started with good intentions and welcome progress. Luce was able to cut down on the pain pills, and she could brush her teeth without wincing and cursing all the way through.

When she came back to the kitchen, Kendra sat with her last coffee before the workday started, reading on her phone. She looked up and smiled at Luce, the kind of smile that made it tempting to forget about work altogether. She missed that new-found intimacy, but they were both still exhausted, absorbing the impact of recent events.

They were doing the best they could, and that wasn't bad at all, she reflected.

"Good morning?" she offered.

"It is. You know, through all of this I've learned that I'm pretty good at giving people advice, not so good at taking it. Look at me, taking a few minutes extra with my coffee. The world doesn't stop."

"No, it doesn't." Luce was about to launch into how she'd come to the same realization, but Kendra made her mind go completely off track when she said,

"And you looking gorgeous doesn't hurt either."

"Come on," Luce protested. At times, Kendra's frank ways of complimenting still made her self-conscious. Flattered, that, too, but self-conscious at the same time.

"I'm a scientist. I give you nothing but the facts."

"You're goofy," Luce declared. "I love that about you."

"Just that?"

Kendra was standing right in front of her, her tone holding a note of challenge. Regardless, the answer was easy.

"I love you," she said, leaning in for a kiss. She had to leave right now, or she wouldn't be able to tear herself away.

Kendra's whispered "love you too" came just in time before her cell phone rang.

Ritter was calling from the station, his tone urgent.

"Are you on your way?"

"I was just about to leave. What happened?"

"A man just walked into a free clinic with a gunshot wound. Doctor told the nurse to call it in, but now he's holding her hostage."

"Fuck. Milano."

"Yes."

"Text me the address. I'll meet you there."

There was no time to think about the eventualities too much.

"You have the keys, so you can just lock the door behind you. I'll see you later."

"Is it going to be dangerous?" Kendra asked, sounding anxious.

Luce wasn't going to sugarcoat reality, especially if she still bore the traces of how far Milano was willing to go.

"He's on his own. This could be over by the time I arrive there, but...I promise you, I'll be careful." Another quick kiss, and she was out the door.

When she arrived, the evacuation of the area around the small clinic was already underway, a reminder of the day she'd met

Kendra, when there had been a credible bomb threat at her workplace.

"Do we know how many are inside? What kind of weapons he has?" Luce asked as she fastened her Kevlar.

"A handgun," Ritter responded curtly. "The nurse over there, Nora Alexander, ushered most of the patients and colleagues out. Milano threatened the doctor and another patient in an exam room."

Luce looked over at the building. The windows were covered by blinds.

"It's the window in the back," Ritter, who had followed her gaze, said. She could see the tactical team getting in position.

She couldn't remember much about that moment other than she'd definitely hit him. Apparently, Milano had managed on his own for a few days, but had come to the end of his line, which likely meant she had given him more than a flesh wound.

They wanted him out for the count, not dead. They still needed him to give up Sarah and Poppy's location.

Her mind flashed back to the children on the construction site, with limited supplies. With Milano on the run in the past few days, how were the two faring?

There was another, more horrific possibility than a lack of supplies, but Luce wasn't ready to go there yet.

A gunshot rang out inside the building, and the tactical team was on the move. Luce and Ritter jogged across the street to follow them inside.

The waiting area was empty as well as a couple of exam rooms and offices that had been left in a hurry.

When Luce and Ritter came to the room where Milano had held the doctor and the patient, a middle-aged man, hostage, it was still in relative chaos.

Milano was on the ground, still fighting as he was being cuffed. One of the members of the tactical team had picked up his weapon, and the damage didn't extend to more than a painting on the wall sporting a bullet hole.

The patient was shaking, and the doctor spoke softly to him.

Luce cast a glance at Milano, not a doubt in her mind that he recognized her when, even injured, he managed a grin.

Her heart sank. This could mean many things, and nothing good for Poppy and Sarah. She blinked, forcing herself to keep her emotions in check.

"Where are they?"

"Fuck you. I'm not talking to you without a lawyer."

Of course.

"Get him out of here," she said brusquely, and he laughed.

"What happened to your face?"

"Shut up," Ritter told him.

Luce held back a smile and turned to the other occupants of the room.

"Is anyone hurt?"

The doctor shook her head. "Mr. Yates was just here for a check-up. This man spoke to Nora, then things got heated and he came barging in...and he—he shot at the painting."

Like Luce, she seemed to be wrestling with the possibilities.

"That was when Ms. Alexander got everyone else out?"

Milano must have been in a lot of pain to panic like that, firing a shot when he should have known it would accelerate things. Luce couldn't say she felt sorry for him.

"Nora, yes. Thank God."

Thanks to Nora's quick thinking too, Luce wasn't going to argue. This was shaping up to be a good day, and she was going to make sure it stayed that way.

"Did you get a chance to look at his wound?" Luce would have liked to haul him into an interrogation room right this minute, but she was aware that it wasn't likely to happen. The sooner they could get some information out of him, the better.

"I'm afraid there was no time, but he was bleeding pretty badly," the doctor said. "I can't tell you for sure, but if I had to guess, he'll probably need surgery."

"Okay. Thank you."

Paramedics joined them to check on the hostages. A couple of them wheeled Milano out on a stretcher.

Luce turned to Ritter.

"Let's go back then. As soon as he has had medical attention, we'll have him make the call. I'm curious to see who will represent him."

They arrived at the station, about to go up in the elevator when the sight nearly made her jaw drop. "I'll join you upstairs," she said to Ritter and walked over to where Kendra was standing with a detective from another unit. Vice, Luce remembered.

"Hey there."

"Luce." Kendra's expression showed a lovable mix of emotions, concern and surprise among them. "I promise I'm not stalking you. The clinic asked me to check on a pregnant patient who's in holding, and Detective Jackson had some questions..." She caught herself. "And I don't think I should be telling you any details. How did it go on your end?"

Reading the room correctly, Jackson excused herself with a smile. "I have to go back. Thank you for coming in, Dr. Jones. Detective Allen."

Luce was aware of Kendra's eyes on her. Still concerned, with a hint of admiration. She realized she was still wearing the Kevlar over her shirt.

"There was some action, but I wasn't close to it. I promise. We got Milano. He'll still need surgery, but I hope we can talk to him soon." She could feel herself breathe easier as some of the stress and tension were falling away, though she couldn't let down her guard yet. Too many critical questions still required answers.

"Sounds good. And I don't know if Detective Jackson will share what I said to her with you. In case she doesn't, there's nothing to worry about. They needed a doctor to check on the woman, and I had the time."

"I'm glad to hear that...and to run into you."

Luce hesitated for a split-second, then she pulled Kendra into a quick embrace.

"I'll see you later."

"After everything, is it possible you'll be home early?" Kendra asked, sounding hopeful.

"I'm not sure yet. Depends on whether we can see Milano before his surgery."

"Okay. You know where to find me."

They shared a quick kiss, and Kendra left. Luce went to join Ritter, and she didn't feel guilty at all for having another coffee—this time, with milk—and a chocolate bar, nothing with nuts.

She was determined to get results—hopefully today.

Chapter Twenty

L uce and Ritter exchanged a look when a less cocky-looking Milano asked for a public defender. They could tell he hadn't expected this turn of events, having been represented by attorneys working for Brock and Dobbs before.

"You said you'd be talking to us with a lawyer present," she said. "Make it quick. Where are Sarah and Poppy? Are they still alive?"

"They were the last time I saw them," he sneered. "The rest, you should maybe ask Mr. Brock."

Her earlier optimism aside, Luce was about to see red, going around in circles with these men for too long.

"You are already wasting time, Mr. Milano. You got one chance to be smart. We know that you cut Brock off from the feed after his arrest. He doesn't know where they are. You were the only one."

"What's in it for me?"

"What's in it for you?" The disbelief came through clearly in Ritter's question. "Mr. Milano, I don't think you fully understand your situation. Your only hope at this time is that Ms. Burke and her daughter are alive."

"Or else? You're going to shoot me? I don't think so. I have something you want. Scratch that, I have a lot more than you could ever imagine, but I need some reassurances. I want a deal."

Luce wanted to shake him, but they couldn't all have what they wanted.

"You know that my colleague and I won't make or even promise you a deal. For us to call the D.A. away from her work, you need to be a lot less vague. And we need to know about Sarah first."

He smiled.

"No. You want to know about Mr. Brock and Mrs. Kendrick first."

"What does that mean? We know he's been pumping money into her opponents' campaign. Campaigns, actually, before you took out one of them with a sex scandal. That was so 2015, right?"

Ritter acknowledged her words with a small smile, before he took over, "We also know that you were suspected of causing Ms. Kendrick's accident. Don't overestimate yourself."

Bobby Milano leaned back in his seat, his grin never wavering. "I think you're still underestimating me, Detectives. Look, none of those guys answered my calls, or helped me out with representation, which is why I'm stuck with this gentleman here."

His lawyer frowned, but didn't comment.

"Anyway, yes, I arranged for the other guy to be caught with a couple of whores."

Luce held his gaze. If it wasn't so important to get the information on the still missing mother and child, she might have told him how bored she was by his attempt to make her flinch. In this room, where she was on the right side of the table, in charge, he seemed smaller.

"I had nothing to do with the car crash though. That was all Brock, and I can prove it. Are you going to call the D.A. now?"

Part of her wanted to jump at the chance, not only to move this forward. If the gamble paid off, Brock would go down not only for hiring Milano to abduct Sarah and Poppy, but they would be safe from him forever.

"Tell me what happened with Francine Kendrick, and I will call her," she said.

⁂

D.A. Troy had come over as soon as she heard what was on the table. Luce still felt like tapping her fingers on said table when Milano kept whispering with his lawyer.

Frustrated, she got up from her chair and joined the D.A. in the observation area.

"I hate to give someone like him anything," Troy remarked. "If he can back up all of this like he says though, Mr. Brock and Congressman Dobbs will have many more questions to answer."

"I hear you, but can we accelerate this somehow?"

"You remember there are people I have to answer to?" Troy sighed. "Aside from his role in the kidnapping, he shot a guy point blank, not to mention what he did to your face. It's a little hard to overlook all that."

"I'm not asking you to overlook anything, I just..." Luce reined in her irritation. This time, it wasn't directed at Troy. She needed them to move forward. She needed something to happen, within the next hour, though she was realistic enough to understand that the facts didn't one hundred percent align with her needs.

"Let me make a few phone calls and see what I can do."

⁂

Be careful what you wish for, rang on her mind. A little less than an hour later, Milano was satisfied with the offer on the table. He wasn't going to avoid a substantial prison sentence, but he'd be in a place better shielded from the influence of the people who had hired him in the first place.

Luce wasn't ready to relax yet. There was no saying what they would find at the location, and the fact that it was Tyler next to her in the driver's seat didn't help.

It wasn't a coincidence that Chomsky had sent the former Homicide detective with her.

"He does seem to want that deal," she said into the silence. "He knows he'll get shit if we don't bring them home alive."

"Hm."

"What does that mean? You saw something else back there?" He had eventually joined the D.A. and observed what had been the last part of Milano's interrogation. For now.

"I didn't say that. I'm not yet sure I'm willing to believe him. Who wants to frame who in this?"

"Ritter is taking a look at that safe deposit box right now. If what Milano said pans out, he gets himself a deal."

"You said that already. In different words, but..."

"Yeah. Sorry. I know it sounds selfish, but I really need something to go my way. This case has been a lot."

Luce wasn't sure why she'd said it, and why now. Testing the waters, perhaps.

"No kidding," he agreed. "I think we'll all be glad if we wrap this up today. Troy and her office will figure out the rest."

They had arrived at the location, a residential area just outside of town, houses spread across the landscape. Luce refrained from the impulse to sigh. The address had to be only a few miles from where they had stood over a dead body a few months ago.

Tyler, of course, remembered it too.

"You're not superstitious, are you?"

Luce believed that when bad things could happen, they likely would. If that made her superstitious, so be it. She didn't have Kendra's faith in humanity.

"I think you were right. We'll believe him once we have what we need."

A squad car parked behind them, and together they walked up to the one-story building.

At first glance, it looked non-descript, like the owners were simply away for an undetermined period, or didn't care much about curb appeal. Blinds were down in all windows.

This wasn't one of Brock's properties, because obviously Brock always meant to get away with what he did, his name never associated with the abduction.

"And the plan was to let them go once Sarah agreed to go back to him."

"That was his plan, yes."

Luce shuddered remembering his tone. Tyler was right. They couldn't trust him.

Inside the house, she thought back to when she first set foot in Sarah Burke's home and saw the breakfast on the table. This property was almost as big, though more modest, and no one had cooked in this kitchen in some time. She could see a thin layer of dust on the shelves and appliances.

There was a bathroom on this floor, and two bedrooms and a closed off living area revealing the house's age.

Their calls for Sarah and Poppy were met with deafening silence. None of the bedrooms looked like anything they'd seen on the feed. What did Milano think he could gain with this? Time? Until when?

Luce didn't think he was naïve enough to think that one of Brock's high-priced lawyers would come for him. In fact, Brock had been angry at him for hiding the children on the construction site and not following the timeline they had agreed upon.

Dobbs? D.A. Troy seemed quite certain that he had dropped Milano a long time ago.

They came to a closet door at the end of the hallway. When Luce opened it, she realized that instead of the expected space, there was another door.

"Sarah!" she called. "Poppy! Are you in there? We're the police."

Everything about this damn case felt like a déjà-vu, but then again, while some criminals were smarter than others, their motives didn't differ that much. Most of the time, women and girls paid the price.

"Can you open the door? We tried, but we couldn't," Sarah answered, and Luce suppressed a relieved sigh.

"Please, step back."

She kicked the door, wincing, but it wouldn't budge. She would shoot the lock if she had to, but that would be a last resort. She didn't want to scare the girl. She examined the lock again, then looked up only to notice the small hook on the wall, with a key on it.

"You've got to be kidding me."

She reached up and tried the key in the lock, then pushed down the handle. The door opened, and they stepped into the room where Burke and her daughter had been held for the last couple of weeks.

Luce held back a gasp. She had seen the room on video, but up close, the similarities were undeniable. Damn Hyde. Damn them all.

"Ms. Burke," Tyler said. "It's good to see you. And you must be Poppy," he addressed the girl half hidden behind Sarah. She nodded.

"Great. I'm Tyler, and this is Luce. We're here to bring you home."

Luce forced herself back to the present, taking in the surroundings. The set-up was similar to where the children had been, a sparse room with a fridge and a few cereal boxes.

"An ambulance is on the way," she said to Sarah Burke who still seemed frozen, and quieter, so Poppy wouldn't overhear, Luce asked, "Are you hurt?"

"No. Just sick and tired of cereal and pudding." She pointed to the door they had come through. "We tried, but there was nothing we could use to open that lock. Of course he wouldn't give us cans, let alone a can opener." Her expression turned grim. "I'm normally not one to sit around. That, I could have used." Frustration turned to concern. "We haven't seen him in a couple of days. Did my ex-husband have him killed? Is Francine okay?"

All of these questions now made a whole lot more sense to Luce than they would have only a few days ago.

"Both Mr. Milano and Mr. Brock are in custody. Why don't we have you and Poppy checked out, and afterwards we'll unravel the whole story? We have plenty of coffee at the station, and we can order any food you like."

Sarah's eyes welled up with tears. "That might sound strange, but I so want to hug you right now." And then she followed through with the impulse. Under the circumstances, Luce didn't mind. She of all people understood the emotion perfectly, but she couldn't afford to give in to it, not yet.

This was the win she'd been hoping for. Sarah and Poppy had a tough road ahead. It could have been so much worse.

Chapter
Twenty-One

Everyone agreed that pizza was an excellent idea. It would be everyone's dinner at the same time. Sarah closed her eyes in bliss at the first sip of coffee. Luce had sprung for the run Ritter had made to the nearby coffee shop, and he had returned with all kinds of delicacies that made Poppy's eyes widen. Now, in the fairly neutral but lighter conference room, she was a little less shy.

Luce had provided her with a few loose sheets and a couple of pens from her desk, and she was enjoying her meal while drawing.

Sarah cast her a fond look before she took another sip of her coffee.

"Thank you so much for everything. This has been a nightmare."

"I can imagine," Luce said softly. Not just a figure of speech. "Can you tell us what happened?"

"Aside from the fact that Bobby Milano walked into our house with a gun and forced us to come with him?"

"You knew him?"

Sarah scoffed. "Of course I know him. He used to hang around my ex-husband, especially after Dobbs didn't want to be seen with him anymore, and that says a lot. If it had been just me...I don't know. But I couldn't risk anything with Poppy around."

"I understand. So, he brought you to this place. Did he ever mention why?"

"He gave me the speech about Gavin wanting me back. I don't know if that's all the reason, but mostly I think it was about punishing me and everyone I love. That's why I was worried about Francine and..."

"Matt Layne."

"You know Matt?" Poppy asked, pausing in her drawing. "He's nice."

"Yes, I've met him," Luce confirmed. "You're right. And he's been very worried about you." She realized that Sarah likely didn't know the part of the story where Brock and Milano had tried to frame Layne for the abduction of twelve third-graders.

"Mr. Layne and Ms. Kendrick will be happy to talk to you when you're ready," Luce brought the conversation back to the matter at hand. "I assume Mr. Brock found out about your relationship? He was angry about it?"

"He was...is delusional," Sarah said darkly. She waited until Poppy had gone back to her drawings, immersed in the activity. "Jealous like you wouldn't believe it. I never cheated on him, but he imagined it constantly. Francine and I weren't even close...We played basketball together for one season in college, and later I gave to her campaign. He was livid about that, calling me a traitor."

"I guess that's when he became involved with Bobby Milano?"

"Oh no, the two go way back. Milano is a weasel. He makes himself irreplaceable, or at least that's what he thinks."

"Milano denies being involved in Ms. Kendrick's accident. What's your opinion?"

Sarah shook her head. "I was horrified when I learned about it, but again, we weren't that close anymore. I did send some flowers. Gavin opened an expensive bottle of whiskey that night." She sighed. "You're probably wondering how I could have ever married him. Same old story. He was younger, charming, I didn't expect any of this to happen. I was trying to keep the peace for Poppy, even after the divorce, and for a while I thought we might be able to make it work. Turns out that to him, we were never separated."

"Did you hear from him at all during your captivity?"

"Except for the message he had Milano deliver, that we could get out the moment I agreed to go back to him? No. And given the fact that Gavin was willing to leave us there with him, I doubt that he'd have upheld his part of the bargain."

Luce doubted that too.

"About Milano..."

"He didn't touch me or Poppy," Sarah read her correctly, her voice barely above a whisper. "He wanted me scared, but I knew that Gavin would have him killed. And Milano probably knew it too. Gavin had found out about Matt, but I think he felt more betrayed about my political contributions. He gave a lot to Dobbs. With all the regulations he promised to kill in return, Gavin would have made a fortune. I think he always thought I slept with Francine too."

Luce didn't like that Milano had been hashing out a deal. At least, his story together with Sarah's would ensure that Brock wouldn't benefit from those policies any longer.

Best case scenario, Dobbs soon wouldn't have power to implement them.

Still a win, though it had required many sacrifices from the wrong people.

"Great job everyone," Chomsky told them after Sarah and Poppy had left, and they were about to wrap up the day. "Go home, take some time. The next few days will be busy."

"Busy with paperwork," Tyler mumbled, making Ritter snicker.

"Have a good evening, everyone." The amusement in her tone left no doubt that she'd overheard the comment. Tyler had a point.

As she walked out, Luce glanced at her watch, wondering if she should call Kendra. They had exchanged a few messages, so Kendra was up to date.

They should perhaps celebrate.

"Everything all right?"

Chomsky had caught up with her, and Luce realized that she was standing in the middle of the parking garage, rather indecisive.

"Yes. This is the best possible outcome," she said.

"For the case, yes. I don't like that one of my detectives ended up in the hospital—again. You're doing all right?" Her tone was light, conversational, but Luce wasn't fooled. She was too tired to come up with white lies too.

"I've been better," she admitted. "But we got the children back, Sarah and her daughter, and the men responsible will face a long list of charges. That makes it hurt a little less."

"It does. I think we all need to take some time to look at the bigger picture of this case. Right now, I'll take a moment to be proud of my people."

When she didn't answer right away, Chomsky added dryly, "That would include you, Detective," making Luce laugh.

"I know. Thank you."

"You're welcome. I'll see you tomorrow."

Luce finally got into her car and pulled out of the parking garage. She wondered if she should have a drink somewhere, then she shook her head. Drinking didn't appeal to her any more than it had before the abduction, hers, Sarah's...She stopped at a supermarket, intent on getting something for tomorrow's breakfast. Browsing the aisles, she picked up a few snacks as well, no wine, and went to the cash register where she winced at the final bill.

Who cared? She had a right to indulge herself on a day like this. Like Chomsky had said, this case would have wide-spread implications, which was a good thing.

A new day was ahead. Celebration. She texted Kendra, *How would you like to go out Friday night?*

The answer came right away. *I'd love that. You have a place in mind?*

Actually, yes. Trust me?

Always.

After that, she took a quick shower and got out just in time to catch the call.

"You don't have to sound so disappointed," Jill said, laughing. "I wanted to hear how you were doing."

"I'm fine. And I haven't forgotten about you. There's a whole story surrounding Sarah's abduction. Looks like everyone lied to us multiple times, but we put it all together with her help. It's a cesspool of corruption."

"Tell me more? Can you?"

"I guess now I can. It's mostly the story of Gavin Brock's megalomaniac ambitions, and the idea that everyone should cater to him. He met Milano during his first job after college, when Milano worked for his then boss, and when Brock made it big, he brought him on bord for the dirty jobs. Milano found Wheeler and the others."

Twenty minutes later, when they were about to end the call, Jill asked, "I was wondering what you were doing on the weekend. Sunday? Josie and I could come by if that's okay with you."

"That's very much okay. We said we would do this. I'm sorry I haven't been able to make time yet."

"No problem, we're doing it now. And thank you. This is quite the story."

"It is," Luce agreed, all of a sudden exhausted. "You helped me too. I really appreciate it. See you Sunday?"

"Sure. We can have a glass and celebrate then."

Luce loved her cousin, but when she was back in her bedroom, putting a robe over her PJs, she was aware of her, maybe misplaced, irritation. Why did everyone think alcohol had to be involved? If she was honest, this wasn't about Jill's innocent comment, or even alcohol per se. Perhaps she just resented people who knew how to apply moderation in their lives—to anything, because Luce seemed to have trouble in that department, especially when it came to work, and lately, food.

The door to the bathroom was still open, and she remembered how, a few days ago, she'd struggled to hide the flashback from Kendra. She shut the door quickly and went downstairs to take another look at her purchases. She was entitled, wasn't she? Everyone thought so.

Luce opened bags and put together a plate, all but giggling when she realized this would be a child's dream snack. Mr. and Mrs. Dennis, Caitlyn's moms, Sarah Burke, they'd certainly allow their kids more sweets for a while.

Luce, on the other hand, was an adult, who didn't have to ask anyone if she wanted to go on a binge.

She carried her plate to the living room where she turned on the TV. Who could stand watching the news without chocolate these days? She took a look at her phone. No other messages. Kendra was probably sleeping right now.

She would see her soon.

Tomorrow, she'd be back at work in an atmosphere that had much improved in recent times. The big picture.

Regardless of all the blessings she was eager to count, her throat tightened. Luce hated to cry, but she had held back the impulse for weeks now, and her guard was no longer up.

She had been able to deal with one thing at a time. The sum of them weighed heavily, even knowing that there were people who cared about her.

She hadn't seen the other women since they had given their respective statements, and that was different anyway. No matter what they shared. She was the cop, the one supposed to protect them, and she had, best she could, under the circumstances.

She wondered if Cory had worn the dress.

If Rachel had stuck to her plan to never eat soup again.

Had they overcome the trauma?

Had Luce?

She put the plate on the table, no longer hungry. She wanted to heal, and she wanted it fast. Maybe she had skipped a few necessary steps along the way.

❦

A few angry entitled men had been charged with multiple crimes. Families had been reunited with their loved ones. And Sunday, Luce would be spending time with Jill and her daughter Josie.

She had high hopes for tonight, though she was aware not all the conversations would be light and easy, but she owed it to Kendra, and herself, to raise the subject.

Luce had made a reservation the night before. Standing in front of her bedroom mirror, she took in her appearance with a critical gaze. Luce didn't wear dresses often, but she had bought this one on a whim, last year, after closing a case. It was simple without frills yet feminine. Understated. She allowed the smile, surprised at the relief she felt. What had she expected?

She was going to pick up Kendra in half an hour, so there wasn't a lot of time to obsess. She cast one last look at herself—she had styled her hair with a bit more effort than she would for a night at a pub, but no make-up. A splash of perfume, everything in the comfort zone.

Kendra, too, was wearing a coat over a dress, waiting for Luce on the sidewalk.

"I have to admit I'm curious," she said after sitting in the passenger's seat. She leaned in for a kiss in greeting. "And congratulations. From what I read online, it's all great news."

"Pretty much. Thank you."

"You're welcome. So, where are we going?"

Luce smiled to herself. "It's a surprise."

They spent the drive in comfortable silence, every moment confirming to Luce that she was making the right decisions. She wasn't going to make mistakes with something this good.

"Wow," Kendra commented when they parked in front of the hotel, and Luce handed the keys to a friendly valet. "This *is* a surprise."

"Good."

They walked up the stairs, and once inside, headed to the restaurant on the left where Luce gave her name to the Maître d' who walked them to a quiet table with a view of the river in the distance.

"You look amazing," Kendra said with a smile, and all of a sudden, Luce worried she might misinterpret the set-up. It would be far too early for anything like that...But no, Kendra knew as well as she did that they were still making themselves at home in their relationship.

"Thank you. You do too...and you are amazing. You have been so patient, and I know it can't have been easy."

"When I was scared for you, that was the hardest part. I've been worried sometimes," Kendra admitted.

The waitress brought their menus and asked about their drinking choices. They decided on a light white wine, just a glass. Not for courage. Luce realized she wanted to get the most pressing issues out of the way before the appetizer.

"I know. And I wanted you to know I'm not taking any of it for granted, because we are together. Especially because of...us, I have made a decision."

She had Kendra's full attention, her gaze calm and open. That made a lot of things easier.

"I don't think it was always fair to you. You had a lot to deal with, and I...I think I need to talk to someone. I tried to make myself believe it was all fine, that being with you would make all the other stuff go away..." Damn it, hadn't she cried enough?

"I understand." Kendra reached across the table to take her hand. "I want you to know I'll be there for you no matter what. This is not a setback. I'm proud of you."

"Thank you. I've realized...I want this. All of it. Us, the job, everything, and for that to happen, I need to be more careful. I..." She cast a quick look at the waitress who stood at a distance, leaving them space. "You don't know this about me, but maybe you guessed. I've never had an eating disorder, but a time or two I came close. I have some work to do."

Kendra squeezed her hand gently. "You've been under a lot of pressure."

"True. But this isn't all I wanted to talk about tonight. First of all, we need to put the poor woman out of her misery and order appetizers."

"I think she won't mind waiting a few more minutes."

"Well, I do. I'm kind of hungry now," Luce admitted. "I promise you I'll be all right. We will be. And I swear I'm not trying to change the subject, but I hope you're okay with the fact that I rented us a room for tonight. Part of the surprise."

"So far it's all perfect," Kendra confirmed, and they finally waved the waitress over.

As close to perfect as it could be. They were going to make it.

About the Author

B arbara Winkes writes sapphic crime drama and Christmas romance. She loves writing characters who get the job done, whether it's stopping a predator or saving cherished traditions—while still making time for love. She lives with her wife in Quebec, Canada.

barbarawinkes.com

Also by Barbara Winkes

Luce Allen Mysteries
In Harm's Way

The Crossing Lines Trilogy
Undercover
Redemption
Vengeance

The Connected Series
Promised to the Queen
Drawn to the Enemy
Tempted by the Protector
Saved by the Heiress

Kelli & Merin Romantic Suspense
Thunder
Rain

Standalone
The Amnesia Project